MARVEL
THOR
RAGNAROK
THE JUNIOR NOVEL

© 2017 MARVEL

Cover design by Ching Chan.

Little, Brown and Company
Hachette Book Group
1290 Avenue of the Americas, New York, NY 10104
Visit us at LBYR.com
marvelkids.com

First Edition: October 2017

Little, Brown and Company is a division of Hachette Book Group, Inc. The Little, Brown name and logo are trademarks of Hachette Book Group, Inc.

The publisher is not responsible for websites (or their content) that are not owned by the publisher.

Library of Congress Control Number 2017946352

ISBNs: 978-0-316-41331-2 (paperback), 978-0-316-41568-2 (Scholastic ed.)
978-0-316-41332-9 (ebook)

Printed in the United States of America

LSC-C

10 9 8 7 6 5 4 3 2

MARVEL
THOR
RAGNAROK
THE JUNIOR NOVEL

ADAPTED BY JIM McCANN

BASED ON THE SCREENPLAY BY ERIC PEARSON

STORY BY CRAIG KYLE & CRISTOPHER YOST AND ERIC PEARSON

PRODUCED BY KEVIN FEIGE, P.G.A.

DIRECTED BY TAIKA WAITITI

LITTLE, BROWN AND COMPANY
New York   Boston

TURN TO PAGE 95 FOR A BONUS STORY FEATURING THOR AND THE HULK!

CHAPTER

First there was the heat. It radiated everywhere—the sound of flames crackling, the smell of sulfur and smoke lingering in the air with every breath.

His breath. That came second. Thor drew in several big breaths as he tried to get his bearings. Every exhale bounced back onto his face quickly, letting him know he was in a confined space. A coffin?

Third were the chains. He was bound head to toe in heavy iron chains. They held him tightly, fastened at his feet. He was shackled, hanging upside down, and a wooden box meant to hold a dead man was all that was separating him from an unknown, raging fire.

In short? Thor had definitely had better days.

He flexed slightly, testing the strength of his bonds. They didn't give. Thor inhaled the hot air into his lungs and flexed with all his Asgardian might. His muscles strained. Suddenly, he felt the chains begin to bend until, with a sharp *CRACK*, they flew off him. With a loud boom, the exploding chains blew open the box, sending pieces of wood splintering in all directions. Thor flipped in midair and landed on the ground below. He was free...or so he thought. Looking around, he realized he had only traded one small cell for a much larger one.

Brushing back his long, tousled blond hair that had become as unruly as his beard of late, Thor surveyed his surroundings. He was in a large cavern. Dark stalactites and stalagmites grew from the ceiling and ground. The walls, though dark in color, seemed to dance. Thor narrowed his gaze and peered closely at the shapes moving across the surfaces, and realized there was fire inside the walls themselves.

With that, Thor understood where he was: Muspelheim. When he turned his attention to the center of the room, his suspicions were confirmed. A large throne rose from the ground. It was dark and foreboding. And it was far too large for the skeletal figure that lay slumped upon its seat. Thor, his armor worn, beard grizzled, and cape slightly torn, wondered how much better he looked than the being before him.

"Demon!" Thor cried out. "Reveal yourself. I have freed myself. Now I seek audience with my captor."

His words echoed through the chamber hall. The skeleton looked at him with its empty eye sockets. No reply.

After a few moments, however, Thor began to hear the sound of rushing wind. The echo became a mocking laughter as it rushed toward the skeleton on the throne. Slowly, fire began to glow from within its bones. Suddenly, there was a fiery aura entirely surrounding the skeleton as it began to sit upright in its throne.

A voice boomed from the skeleton. "The son of Odin wishes to see me?"

"Well, that is certainly an improvement," Thor noted, a wry smile crossing his face.

"You may have escaped your prison, but you shall never escape Muspelheim alive." The skeleton laughed at Thor.

"Even after being held captive and strung upside down, I believe I can handle a bag of bones such as yourself," Thor replied.

Just then—from the walls, the ceiling, the floor—the

entire cave lit up as the skeleton caught fire and began to grow. It expanded in size, filling the throne and transforming into a deadly creature of pure flame. It leaned forward and continued laughing at Thor, its maw gaping wide open with evil mirth.

Thor gazed upon his captor, recognizing his fire-filled countenance, though he hadn't before. "Surtur. At last. This look suits you much better, I must say."

"You dare mock me in my own chambers?" Flames shot out in all directions at Surtur's wrath. He rose from his throne, a flaming giant towering above Thor. "I was to bring you to Odin when I returned to Asgard and show him how far his son had fallen. I had hoped to return you alive, but no matter. With or without you, I shall retrieve the Eternal Flame stolen from me by Odin centuries ago."

"I haven't been back to Asgard in some time, but I doubt my father would strike such a deal. That Flame is locked deep away for the protection of the Nine Realms." Thor began to smile.

"I see no reason for you to smile, son of Odin," Surtur growled. "You have no hope of escape."

A slight pounding began to thud, coming closer and

closer. Looking around, Surtur's eyes widened. "What is that sound?"

Thor's smirk expanded into a wide grin, and he held out his arm. "Hope."

With that, the ground below him exploded, and his trusted hammer, Mjolnir, flew into his outstretched hand.

"You wish to return to Asgard, demon? I shall bring you myself." Thor crouched, holding his hammer close to his side, about to leap. With a mighty flex of his powerful legs, he launched himself directly at Surtur. "No need for all of you to come, though. Just your skull!"

With a swift movement, Thor swung Mjolnir and connected with Surtur's jaw in a powerful uppercut, knocking the demon back and off his feet. Thor landed deftly on the ground, readying himself for another attack. Surtur roared in shock and pain. Flames began to grow around him as he summoned the fire. With a gesture of one bony, flame-encased hand, the wall of fire went flying directly at Thor.

Thor began to spin Mjolnir, faster and faster, whipping up a windstorm. The wind created a protective dome around him as the flames from Surtur's attack passed by him. The wind extinguished another attack as Surtur hurled a fireball at Thor. The fire demon became more and more enraged.

Without warning, Thor ran toward the giant Fire Lord, and at the very last second, slid between his legs. Swinging his arm, he used Mjolnir to knock Surtur's knobby knees out from under him, causing the villain to fall to the ground with a scream.

Thor stood above him, holding Mjolnir.

"The next time you wish to see Asgard, do not use the god of thunder as your bargaining chip. Even flames can burn, Surtur." With that, he lifted Mjolnir high, and the air around him began to crackle. Then, from above, a magnificent bolt of lightning surrounded Surtur and struck Thor's foe in the chest. Surtur screamed in agony.

Thor stood above the Fire Lord's head, ready to deliver the final blow, when something caught his attention in the walls. It was one pair of eyes, and then another, and another. Dozens of eyes began to flicker. The flames that had seemed earlier to dance in the walls suddenly gained form. Humanoid fire demons appeared and began to spill from the walls in droves! A screeching noise caused Thor to look up and see the demons descending from the ceiling as well. He felt the burning touch as more grew from the floor, grabbing at his legs.

Thor's shock wore off quickly as he turned to face his foes, who greatly outnumbered him. "Your father has fallen, yet the minions come forth to try and finish what he could not? Sorry, but I am done playing games here."

Looking up, Thor cried to the heavens, "Heimdall! The Bifrost, please," expecting the usual beam of rainbow energy to appear and transport Thor onto the bridge that allowed passage out of and into Asgard. But there was nothing.

Thor cried out again to his friend on Asgard who controlled the bridge. "Heimdall? Heimdall?!"

The demons rushed Thor and quickly engulfed him, piling upon him two stories high. They cackled in their apparent victory. Thor's echoes pleading for the Bifrost rang plaintively through the halls of Surtur's lair, unanswered.

CHAPTER

The Rainbow Bridge of the Bifrost, which looked out onto almost all of creation itself, linking each of the Nine Realms, gleamed brightly with cosmic energy. The gilded domed observatory, from where the bridge originated, rose out of a platform at the edge of Asgard. The bridge itself spilled forth from a giant opening, usually guarded by Heimdall, the all-seeing, all-hearing Asgardian who normally directed it with a powerful sword in the center of the dome.

But at the moment, the sword that opened the Bifrost was missing. And so was Heimdall.

A glow from the center of the Bifrost's controls, which Heimdall would have activated to bring those in need back to Asgard via the Bifrost's magical properties, pulsed. And pulsed. And pulsed.

"This?" said a voice from just outside the dome. "This is only one of the most powerful items in all the Realms. And Odin has entrusted *me* with it."

The voice did not belong to the mighty Heimdall, who never left his post. Instead, a bald man with a slight sneer that was meant to be a smile was showing off to two Asgardian women. "'Skurge,' Odin said to me, 'you are far more suited to guard the entrance to Asgard than that traitor Heimdall,'" the man bragged. "That's when he gave me this sword."

"You must be a brave man to be given such a great responsibility," one of the Asgardian women said. Pleased with himself, Skurge thought that his attempts to impress them were clearly working.

"Oh, the battles I've seen. They would chill your blood. The beasts on Vanaheim had four heads each. Yet I stood my ground and fought them back. I believe that's why he rewarded me." Skurge smiled. "Come, let me show you a view like you've never seen before."

With that, Skurge and the two women continued on,

none of them noticing the beacon pulsing insistently, someone clearly calling on the Bifrost for assistance.

In Muspelheim, a mound of fire demons continued to pile onto the spot where Thor once stood. Surtur began to recover from the bolt of lightning to his chest and rose from the ground, emitting a shriek of glee. His laughter was cut short, though, as the outer ring of fire demons was suddenly flung backward off the pile, shaken by a rumbling. Without warning, Mjolnir burst forth from the top of the mound, sending fire demons flying in a volcanic fashion.

The hammer flew around the room, ricocheting off the walls and ceiling, knocking back fire demons left and right. Surtur watched in horror as victory was seemingly once again snatched away from him. He ducked as the hammer flew back toward where the fire demons had overpowered Thor, only to see the Asgardian standing there, no worse for wear, catching Mjolnir in one outstretched hand as it returned to its owner.

"I believe my visit to your realm has come to an end, Surtur. I prefer milder climes." Swinging Mjolnir, Thor flew up and burst through the top of the cavern.

Thor landed heavily on the ground and once more called out to Heimdall for the Bifrost. He was perplexed. Never had his request been denied; his friend was always at the ready to send him the means needed to return to Asgard. His thoughts were interrupted by a rumbling sound. Perhaps it was the Bifrost, opening to him at last? Turning, he saw the source of the noise, and his heart sank.

Where he'd hoped a beam of energy would alight from above and envelop him to take him home stood a mighty fire dragon, easily one hundred feet long and full of rage. The beast bellowed, and flames shot forth. Thor jumped out of the way to dodge the attack and, directing Mjolnir toward the sky, flew upward to escape the beast's wrath. But the dragon took to the skies to follow the hero. Thor dodged burst after burst of flames that shot forth from the dragon's mouth.

Swiftly, Thor spun in the air and charged the dragon. Catching it off guard, he delivered a blow that knocked the dragon backward. As the dragon fell, Thor continued to pummel it as it crashed into the ground. At last, back on Muspelheim's surface and standing above the dragon, Thor held Mjolnir over the defeated creature's head.

"Only those worthy may lift the mighty hammer

Mjolnir, foul demon-spawn." He dropped the hammer on the dragon's head. Struggling, it could not raise its head from under Mjolnir. "Clearly, you are not worthy."

Thor turned his attention to the heavens once more. "Heimdall! The Bifrost, please. I am quite finished here." He waited a moment, but nothing. His attention turned away from the dragon, he didn't notice the beast slowly begin to swish its deadly tail.

"That was beautiful," marveled one of the Asgardian women as they reentered the dome of the Bifrost.

"Oh." Skurge chuckled. "That was nothing. I have an even better view for you if you ladies wish to join me—"

The other woman pointed at the pulsing from the Bifrost controls. "Is that normal?"

Skurge paled. "*Uhhhhh*, of course. Yes. You are"—he frantically searched for the sword that controlled the Bifrost, which he had carelessly tossed into a corner after he'd finished displaying it to the women—"are about to see...Ah! There it is!" He grabbed the sword and ran to the controls. "Would you like to see the Bifrost in action?" His face contorted into his version of a smile as he inserted the sword and turned it. The Bifrost's center began to spin as its immense energy powered up.

"Whoof!" Thor was knocked off his feet by the dragon's tail. The beast had been inching ever closer as Thor waited for the Bifrost and Heimdall. Suddenly, his face was mouth level with the dragon. He saw flames begin to form. Grabbing Mjolnir, Thor leaped from the ground seconds before being burned to a crisp, and took to the skies once more.

The dragon, now freed from the hammer's weight, followed in pursuit. Ahead, Thor at last spotted the familiar swirling of Bifrost energy. It was about time! He sped up, the dragon fast on his heels. As the opening cleared, Thor zoomed through it. The dragon's head entered the Bifrost a second later.

"Are you ready to witness something none but the luckiest on Asgard have ever seen?" Skurge was almost sweating with excitement and the chance to brag before two of the most beautiful Asgardians he had ever entertained. This Keeper-of-the-Bifrost thing sure did have its perks.

The Bifrost opened, and immediately Thor came flying through!

"Close it! The Bifrost! Now!" Thor bellowed, sliding to a halt in the center of the dome. As Skurge twisted the control, the head of the flame dragon entered through the Bifrost... and was quickly severed from its body by the gate's closing. The decapitated head slid across the floor of the dome and landed at the feet of the two women, who screamed and promptly fled.

Thor could barely contain his rage as he turned on this stranger before him. Standing at full height, covered in dragon's blood and singed from his fight with the fire demons, he strode toward Skurge. "Who are you and where is Heimdall?"

Skurge tried to stand tall, but the sight before him made his spine and legs not want to cooperate. He cleared his throat, attempting to speak with some authority. "I— I am Skurge, Keeper of... of the Bifrost."

"Some 'Keeper' you are. Did you not hear my many calls?" Thor was nearly toe-to-toe with the Asgardian, who was still attempting to remain brave.

"I was... attending to other business."

"So I saw." Thor looked around. "You claim to be the Keeper; where is Heimdall?"

Skurge scoffed before he could stop himself. "That traitor? Banished."

"Traitor? Heimdall? Never! Who laid such claims?" Thor was shocked.

Skurge smiled. This was the one part he liked to say to anyone who would listen. "Why, by Odin himself. And it was Odin who named me Keeper of the Bifrost, as reward for my service and—"

"Odin? I think not," Thor interrupted. He turned and flew off in the direction of the palace.

Skurge ran after Thor but slipped in a puddle of dragon gore. "Wait! Only I can announce you to Odin! 'Tis his orders!" Covered in muck, Skurge gave up trying to run after Thor, who was by then but a small dot on the horizon of Asgard.

Skurge groaned. He hoped he wouldn't lose his job because of this.

CHAPTER

And so Loki, ever clever, was able to outwit the Dark Elf Malekith and save all of Asgard, though it meant sacrificing his life for his home, his father, and all the Nine Realms. The end."

A chorus of clapping rose from the considerable crowd grouped around the stage. An actor was narrating a play being performed in the middle of a grand terrace to an audience filled with rapt Asgardians. At the head of the makeshift open-air theater, seated upon a massive throne, was Odin, lounging off to one side as he drank a goblet of wine.

"And destroyed the Aether, ending the Convergence. We mustn't forget that detail, mustn't we?" Odin directed from the throne.

The narrator nodded eagerly but, before he could revise the ending, a murmur rose from the crowd and grew in scale until the audience was positively atwitter. Odin turned, annoyed at the disturbance, and his heart sank.

Headed straight toward him was Thor. His gaze was trained on Odin as he strode through the parting crowd, all of whom were murmuring about his return...and his appearance.

"Father, I would have words with thee," Thor addressed Odin.

"Thor! Um, son!" Odin sat up straight suddenly, composing himself. "What an...unexpected honor to have you return. You've just missed the most marvelous play about the life of your poor, fallen adopted brother, Loki."

"It seems I have missed much," Thor returned pointedly, glowering at Odin.

"You're right. We should amend the ending to include Thor's role in the Great Battle," Odin said to the royal scribe, who was making notes on the play. He turned back to Thor. "Would you like to see the revisions, my son?"

"I heard enough already, thank you, Father." Thor began to approach the throne. Odin waved his hands, and members of the Einherjar, his Royal Knights, escorted the citizens off the terrace, allowing for privacy between the two.

"It has been far too long since I have seen you, son."

"And I, you, it appears," Thor said.

"I must say, are you unwell? Because you look rather unlike yourself." Odin waved his hand at Thor's haggard, dragon blood–soaked appearance.

Thor gave a wry smile. "Funny, I was going to say the same about you, Father."

Odin shifted uncomfortably in his seat for a moment before suddenly standing and starting to make his way off the terrace. "Please, clean up and join me for, ah, supper. Wouldn't that be grand?"

Thor leaped up and landed in front of Odin, blocking his path to the door. "You know my favorite thing about travels? The return home. It's like Mjolnir. No matter how far I throw it, it shall always return to my hand, even if something is in the way." Thor lifted Mjolnir high in his hand as though to throw it straight through Odin.

"Now, wait there just a moment, son—"

Thor began to swing Mjolnir around his head, whipping it into a faster and faster frenzy until the hammer was poised for release.

"All right, all right!" Odin cried out. There was a tense beat, and then "Odin" began to fade. When the illusion was gone, Loki stood in its place!

Thor shook his head in disbelief. "I wanted to be wrong about you, brother. How did you escape death?"

"By evading its grasp in the first place, of course." Loki sneered at his adopted brother.

"Only you would make a mockery of your own sacrifice. I believed you'd changed, Loki. I believed you to be good and decent in the end." Thor was genuinely upset by uncovering this latest deceit in his brother's endless list of mischief and troubles.

"And I believed in unicorns and candy fountains, but some things are impossible, aren't they? Now, can we skip the sanctimonious lecture about how I fooled you yet again and get to the point I know you're *dying* to make, so you can go and shower at the very least?" Loki turned up his nose in disgust to emphasize his point.

"I nearly died thanks to your treachery and that buffoon you placed at the helm of the Bifrost. Where is Heimdall?"

Loki shrugged. "Wherever those who their king declares traitors and relieves them of duty go, I suppose."

"And where is Father?" Thor asked through gritted teeth.

"That *is* the question, isn't it?" Loki mused, smiling.

Thor balled his Mjolnir-free hand into a fist. "Now is not the time for tricks, Loki. I have felt something—something dark coming—and we need Father."

"Do we really, though? I've managed quite well while you've been gone and he's been...off." Loki was quite pleased with himself as a ruler.

"Take me to him now or I shall have Mjolnir meet the back of your head," Thor said, growling.

"That is one incentive, I suppose. But I assure you, there's nothing to fear. Asgard is as safe as it has ever been."

Thor's face darkened. "We must find Father to ensure that."

At the entrance to the Bifrost, Thor and Loki stood ready for the portal to be opened and transport them to wherever Loki was hiding Odin.

Loki moved toward Skurge and hissed, "I gave you one job! Keep my brother away."

Skurge shook visibly. "I'm sorry, Your Highness. But

there was…" He looked over his shoulder at the decapitated dragon's head in the corner of the observatory.

Loki turned to Thor. "Bringing home souvenirs now, brother?"

"I'm thinking of collecting heads and having them mounted on my wall. Care to join my newest trophy?" Thor retorted.

"My, my. Such hostility. Asgard was certainly much more peaceful when I was in charge." Loki loved needling his brother and reveled in the annoyance it caused. Thor, however, merely waved off his heckling today, focusing on other, more important matters.

"You—Skurp," he called out.

"It's Skurge, actually," the Asgardian replied.

"There is something not right in the universe, and I fear it is headed toward Asgard. While we are gone, entertain yourself by performing the task at hand, rather than with wine and women." Thor was clearly not pleased that Heimdall was missing. "I've brought backup for you."

Thor nodded to the entrance of the Bifrost observatory dome. Standing there, nearly filling the doorway, were Volstagg and Fandral, Thor's most trusted friends in life and battle. Skurge's jaw dropped open. "Two of the Warriors Three? I fought with you at Vanaheim." He walked toward the duo, hand outstretched. "Skurge. It's an honor," he said. Volstagg pulled a mop from behind his back and placed it firmly in Skurge's hand.

Fandral looked at the humbled Skurge. "It is time to clean house, I believe." He nodded to the dragon's head.

Volstagg laughed. "And don't miss a spot. Fandral is very particular."

The Bifrost powered up, and a swirling portal opened. "Time to go, brother. Unless you have any other duties to assign?" Loki stepped through it.

Fandral looked to Thor. "Do not worry, Odinson. We will be here to ensure your safe return. Even if Volstagg has to sit on this cretin to do it."

"We fought together," Skurge muttered sadly under his breath.

Thor grasped his friend's hand in thanks and, with a final warning glare in Skurge's direction, vanished into the Bifrost.

CHAPTER

Several rats were scampering over the remains of a carton of discarded rotting fruit, when a pair of feet wearing three pairs of socks and ragged shoes shuffled by, scaring them off. The alley was just off Thirty-Seventh Street in New York City's Flower District, a name that conveyed far more beauty than what actually met the eye if one looked closely enough into the abandoned and darkened spaces between buildings. The littered alleys held dumpsters full of fruits and vegetables that had been fresh the day before but gone bad in the afternoon heat. By morning, they'd been thrown out and left for the forgotten beggars and animals to duke it out for that day's meal.

The man who'd scared off the rats wore tattered

clothes and looked as though he hadn't bathed in days. A torn cloth covered his right eye. He rummaged through a dumpster and found a bunch of bananas, still perfectly wrapped. It was his lucky day!

He was tucking the almost-fresh produce into one of his many layers when a blinding light overpowered the dawn glow of the alley. When his eye adjusted, he saw two men approaching him. The man quickly glanced down and, spotting an abandoned piece of wood, picked it up and raised it like a sword.

"Stand and hold, foul ones. I was a great warrior in my day, and I still know how to wield a weapon." He began to swing the piece of wood at the men, who stepped back, surprised.

Thor looked at his brother in confusion and spoke in a low tone. "New York? Why here, brother? And why show me this poor lost soul?"

They were dressed in regular Earth street wear—shirts and slacks—and Thor carried an umbrella. His hair was swept back into a ponytail. Loki's magic was projecting an illusion onto the duo.

Loki motioned for Thor to look again at their "attacker." Thor closely inspected the old man approaching them and spouting gibberish. But the man stood tall for a moment, his hair brushed back, and it was then that Thor saw the telltale bandage covering one eye.

Before them stood no ordinary man: This was Odin, king of Asgard!

Thor's stomach dropped in sorrow and pity. "I shall never forgive you for this," he hissed at Loki as he approached the agitated man, his arms held out, trying to calm him.

"Back! Back, I say!" cried Odin.

"Father." Thor's voice cracked with emotion. "It is I, Thor." The disheveled man stopped midswing. "Yes, Thor, your son. And this, the other I bring with me, is Loki."

"Thor. Loki." The man mumbled the words, a faint memory stirring as these names poked at something within him, but he couldn't quite grasp it.

"Yes, Father. And you are Odin, the king of Asgard and protector of the Nine Realms," Thor continued, hoping to reach through the magic-induced amnesiac fog that clouded his father's mind.

"Asgard." This struck a chord with the man. "Asgard," he repeated. "Home?"

Thor nearly wept. "Yes, Father, Asgard is your home, and I've come to bring you back and place you on the throne as its rightful ruler."

The man pushed back a strand of hair from his one good eye as he studied Thor, and a spark of familiarity lit the clouded blue. He dropped the piece of wood, and a tear formed in his eye.

"Thor? Loki? My sons." He held out his arms. "My sons!" His voice grew stronger as he embraced Thor. Loki turned away, partly in shame at his actions that had put Odin in this situation, and partly in shock at being called *son* by Odin.

Thor held his father gently. The once-formidable ruler was so frail Thor could have carried him with one hand. How far his father had fallen under Loki's trickery! He wondered how long his father had suffered in these conditions.

"I'm sorry, Father. I never should have left. But come, we shall return, all *three* of us." Thor looked pointedly at Loki as if to say, *Don't even think about disappearing your way out of this one.* Thor was helping to steady his father, who was gazing into his eyes.

As Thor was holding Odin, he felt the power of the

All-Seeing One slowly reach Odin even in his weakened state.

"Tell me, my boy. What has you frightened so?"

"A feeling, Father. A darkness I cannot escape. I feel it has chased me, or I it, across the Realms for months now. I went to Muspelheim, thinking that the fire demon Surtur was the cause, but he knew nothing." Thor looked into his father's eye, hoping there would be some flicker of knowledge or recognition.

Odin pushed his son away and grabbed his head, crying out in pain and falling to the ground. It seemed Thor had probed too deeply into long-buried memories and caused his father such pain.

Thor turned to Loki, apoplectic with rage. "You cast him out, made him forget who he was. Now he cannot remember even the stories he told us as warnings!" Thor's face reddened. "Tell me, Loki, was this necessary? How could even you do something so foul?"

Loki shrugged, trying to remain calm. "I did what I thought best. Maybe you wouldn't have done the same, but you never cared for the throne anyway."

"Stories. The throne." Odin was struggling to right himself. Thor rushed to his father's side. "Hela." The word hung in the air like a shadow, chilling all three men in the alley to their bones.

"Hela? She is but a myth, Father. Stories told to frighten children." Thor helped his father to his feet.

"Odinson." Thor looked at his father as Odin called him the name he felt he'd run from most of his adult life. "You are the Odinson. It is *you* who must return to Asgard, and quickly."

Thor shook his head. "No, Father. You are the rightful one to be seated on the throne. I am no king."

Odin grabbed him. "You must become one now, my son. This place, Asgard...all of the Nine Realms need the Odinson to sit on the throne. Asgard needs its king, my child, and that is you."

Loki cleared his throat. "If I may, Asgard has flourished quite well under the reign of its current king. I don't see—"

Thor's steely look silenced Loki. Turning his gaze back to his father, he said, "This darkness I have felt and Hela, are they connected?"

Odin swatted at invisible foes that plagued his now-damaged mind. "The Odinson is needed on Asgard," he uttered at last. "If the darkness is coming, it will need protecting."

"Then we shall protect it together, the two of us, Thor and Odin," Thor said, lifting his umbrella. He struck it to the ground, and suddenly he and Loki were dressed in their Asgardian clothes and armor. His father remained in tatters. "Come, Father. It is time to return you to your place."

He looked to Loki, who nodded.

"Skurge, the Bifrost, if you will," Thor called out. "Oh, and we have company," he added, looking at his father.

The energy from the Bifrost beamed down and covered the trio, and in an instant, they were whisked out of the alley in New York City. The rats scurried from the shadows and began fighting over the bundle of fresh bananas Odin had left behind.

In the storm of the Bifrost, Thor helped Odin as they raced toward Asgard. Loki was ahead of them, trying to not think of the many unpleasant punishments his brother and father must have in mind for him for when they returned to Asgard. So deep in thought was Loki that he failed to notice the subtle tremor that rocked the Bifrost slightly.

Looking ahead at his brother, Thor wondered if perhaps

he was seeing one of Loki's illusions. Could the Bifrost actually be shaking? Before he could ask, he saw black tendrils suddenly wrap themselves around the Bifrost before him. He looked back, and more tendrils were quickly creeping through, gaining on Thor and Odin.

"Brother!" Thor called out a warning, but Loki turned to him a moment too late. The tendrils seemed to be moving through the Bifrost and cutting off the trio from their destination. One dark talon from the tendrils reached out for Loki.

It found its mark and hit Loki square in his helmet, knocking him to the Bifrost's edge. Loki struggled to stay conscious, but everywhere he looked, there seemed to be darkness.

Loki fell from the portal.

"No!" screamed Thor as he watched his brother being thrown from the Bifrost into the blackness of the cosmos below. He let go of his father briefly as he struggled to spot Loki. There was no sign of his brother.

The Bifrost shook again. With a sense of dread, Thor turned back, too late to act. The black tendrils had made their way up and now grasped Odin.

"Father!" Thor's cries seemed to be swallowed by the darkness that was covering the Bifrost.

"You are...the Odinson...." His father's words hung in the air as Odin was pulled from the Bifrost and hurled back toward Earth.

With a roar, Thor hurled Mjolnir at the dark tendrils to drive them back. His trusted hammer cut through the blackness, revealing that Odin was no longer there. Before it could return to Thor's hand, the dark tendrils closed around Mjolnir, and it, too, vanished.

Thor was alone and weaponless on the Bifrost, his father and brother both missing and darkness closing in fast upon him. He adopted a fighting stance as best he could, ready to attack his unseen foe with his fists if needed. "Come at me, then! Do your worst!"

As if answering his dare, the Bifrost shook with a great heave, and Thor was knocked off course. The darkness that had been plaguing him for months seemed to form before him as one last tremor hurled him off the Bifrost.

He fell into nothingness, watching the darkness retreat from the Bifrost as his own darkness began to overtake him, and he lost consciousness.

In the Bifrost observatory, Skurge, who had been left alone to clean after Fandral and Volstagg had activated the Bifrost for Thor, paused in his mopping to look back at the Rainbow Bridge. To his surprise, there was no sign of anyone. He shrugged and was about to turn away when he saw the most terrifyingly beautiful figure begin to appear from black tendrils at the far end of the Bifrost and advance toward him.

CHAPTER

Thor's eyes snapped open. He felt heavier than normal, the air thicker, dusty. He was not on the Bifrost nor on Asgard nor Earth. Even before looking around, Thor knew this place felt different from any world he'd ever been to.

Sitting up slowly, he took in his surroundings. The desolate landscape was littered, quite literally, with debris: Broken pieces of ships, wheels, cracked weapons, and other trash were piled everywhere. Thor glanced up and gasped. Where there should have been stars or a clear sky were instead hundreds of wormholes filling the air. Occasionally, more debris would fall through one of the holes and crash to the ground. A broken spaceship came spilling out of a wormhole nearby, and he watched as strange aliens hurriedly made their way in its direction. *Scavengers*, he thought.

Looking above him once again, Thor saw that the smaller wormholes were dwarfed by one massive wormhole, this one a deeper color than the rest and occasionally lighting up as if electricity was coursing through it.

As he struggled to gain his bearings, a square ship hovered its way toward him. It reached nearer and suddenly broke apart into four smaller ships, which descended and surrounded him. Before he could act, a pair of grotesque aliens exited each ship and aimed their weapons at him.

"Hold!" he cried, hands up. "I am not your foe."

Ignoring him, the aliens fired all at once. With a jolt, energy coursed through Thor as he was wrapped in electrical netting from all sides, knocking him onto his back. He couldn't speak or move as the aliens closed in.

Something caught Thor's attention in the air above the aliens. A sleek ship, one well cared for and vastly different from the ones the aliens had descended from, came to a halt, hovering above them. The top slid open, and out jumped...a woman! This was no ordinary woman. Her helmet revealed her face and she was smiling, apparently ready to enjoy the fight about to ensue.

As she landed, she knocked out two aliens with one punch from her brass-knuckled fist. She turned and kicked away two more. The bracers that laced up her forearms began to expand as though alive, and covered her entire forearm and fist. Suddenly, an armored fist shot from her hand and mimicked her gestures, grasping the last fleeing alien by the foot, picking him up, and slamming him to the ground. The armor retracted to her fist, and her bracers diminished, returning to their original design on her arms.

The netting that held Thor still sent shock waves through his body, making it difficult for him to talk and impossible to move. Nevertheless, he smiled. He recognized what this woman was.

"You...are...Valkyrie." He smiled, speaking through the pain of the electricity coursing through his body. The Valkyrie were some of Asgard's fiercest warriors. He tried to reach out to his savior. "I...am...Thor. Son of... Odin."

"And I care because...?" The woman clearly did not. She sneered down at him.

"Please...for Asgard...free me. Help me return. There...is a darkness." Thor wondered why the woman was not moving to unbind him. He began to struggle against the netting, ignoring the pain that every movement brought on as he was shocked again and again.

"You're not on Asgard anymore, and there's plenty of darkness here, so get used to it," Valkyrie said, spitting out the word *Asgard*.

Thor finally managed to free one arm. He reached out and nearly grabbed her leg in desperation. Valkyrie swiftly sidestepped him and kicked his hand away.

"You don't understand...." Thor tried again weakly.

"Oh, that's where you have it wrong. I understand perfectly." She aimed a small device at him, and a disk shot out of it, embedding itself into Thor's chest. She took out a fob control, pushed a button, and sent a jolt through Thor.

The pain that ran through him was unlike anything he'd ever felt. Thor's whole body stiffened, paralyzed. Still looking up at the woman, he muttered one last plea.

"For...Asgard..." His voice was raspy, as even his vocal cords began to stiffen along with the rest of him.

With a final swift kick to his head, Valkyrie knocked out Thor. She looked down at him. If she was surprised to see an Asgardian on this dismal planet, it didn't register on her face. Then again, she was not known for showing emotion. Getting the job done was her specialty.

She loaded Thor onto her ship and slid behind the controls. Taking out a communicator, she adjusted the dial and spoke into it. "Scrapper 142 reporting in. I have new cargo. Tell him to expect me soon. He'll want this one." She clicked off the communicator and looked back at the unconscious Thor.

"Welcome to Sakaar, son of Odin." With that, she shifted the controls and her ship rose from the ground, banked away from the scavengers below, and headed to the city in the distance.

Back on Asgard, the Bifrost had barely finished breaking apart when the dark tendrils began to spill out of the observatory. They traveled to an overlook of the majestic land and swirled to form a single mass, taking on a humanoid figure. As Asgardians watched, the Einherjar marched out in force to face this mysterious threat. Within moments, the blackness had cleared away, and in its place stood a woman.

It was clear this was no ordinary woman. Dressed in a leathery armor of black and green, with long black hair and an icy-cold look in her heavily shadowed eyes, the woman surveyed the realm before her. A hush fell over all Asgard as it held its collective breath, waiting for her to speak.

When her voice sounded at last, it rang out clear and strong, full of authority in a tone that brooked no room for dissent. "I have returned, although most of you know me as a nightmare or fable. But I assure you, I am no tale. I am Hela, queen of Hel, ruler of the Underworld. Long ago, I was cast out of Asgard by Odin and his warriors, but my time to return has arrived. You are without a king on the throne. It is not the throne I seek, however. It is the end of Asgard itself. My name was once whispered as a possibility, a foretelling of events that could lead to the fall of your beloved realm."

Hela began descending the stairs from her overlook. The Einherjar readied their swords, spears, and shields to protect the citizens of Asgard.

"I am no whisper. I am no possibility," Hela announced, her voice growing louder, like an approaching storm. She paused, and every Asgardian felt she was looking directly into their fearful souls.

"I am an inevitability."

With that, she raised her arms, and the entirety of the Einherjar were defeated with one fell swoop of the dark tendrils. The people of Asgard inhaled a collective gasp of panic and began to run frantically every which way, desperate to escape the evil that had descended upon their realm.

"Flee. Find shelter if you can." Hela's voice echoed through the land. "It matters not." With a tilt of her head, fires sprang up all around.

"I am the ruler of Death, and I assure this: Asgard is dead."

CHAPTER

With its vibrant colors and eclectic decor, the Grandmaster's chamber was nearly as unique as its owner.

Nearly.

Seated on a plush couch, the Grandmaster, the ruler of all Sakaar, sipped a steaming beverage from a golden goblet.

"It looks like it's scalding hot, but it's actually quite refreshingly cool. That's the magic. Isn't it great?" He surveyed the room. His two handmaidens nodded in agreement obediently, while a sulking figure in the corner simply rolled her eyes in boredom. The rest of the room was filled with the highest of Sakaarian society. They were dressed in their culture's finest formal wear, creating a sea of glittering colors and jewels. They all nodded enthusiastically at the Grandmaster's proclamation of his drink's unique form and taste, and began motioning to the servants, ordering these deceptive beverages for themselves. The Grandmaster sipped, smiling at the fact that he was, quite literally, a tastemaker. His delight with his beverage was interrupted, however, by a zapping noise, followed by a stifled cry of pain making its way toward his chamber.

"This...*ungg*...really isn't necessary, is it?" came a voice from the hallway as Valkyrie entered the chamber. Behind her, Thor struggled to follow as he was repeatedly shocked by the disk Valkyrie had attached to his chest.

The Grandmaster clapped twice and the room fell silent, all eyes on the brawny newcomer now felled to his knees at the center of the opulent chamber. The Grandmaster looked closely at Thor. "A bit ragged, don't you think? But even diamonds start as coal, I guess." Turning his attention to Valkyrie, he asked, "What have you brought me?"

"A contender." Her curt reply was followed by her casual push of a button on her control, jolting Thor again, causing him to flex in response.

"Yes, yes. Real potential, I see. A little makeover and the crowd will eat him up. Very nice, Scrapper 142. Wouldn't you agree, Topaz?"

The sulking figure in the corner gave only an icy stare in response. Valkyrie smiled slightly at her rival. "Don't worry; I'm sure you'll find your own contender. That is, if you ever get up and actually search for one," she muttered under her breath, but loudly enough for Topaz—and the rest of the room—to hear.

The Grandmaster waved his hands benevolently, setting his beloved drink down delicately on its gilded saucer. "Ladies, please. This is a place of enjoyment and relaxation. No need for feuds. We leave that to the arena."

At the sound of the word, Thor looked at the Grandmaster. "What arena?"

"What arena?" The Grandmaster chuckled. "Oh, Scrapper 142, this really is quite fresh meat."

"Which I expect to be paid for," she replied smartly, her hand outstretched.

"Yes, yes. Your bounty." The Grandmaster snapped his fingers, and a servant brought forth a bag of coins.

Valkyrie stared at the bag, then at the Grandmaster. "Double for this one. Trust me. He's worth it."

The Grandmaster sighed and snapped again, and another servant brought a second bag. "What makes you so sure? I'm practically dying to know."

"Ask him yourself." Then Valkyrie turned and left the chamber, but not before giving Topaz a sly grin. They clearly had an unspoken contest between them, and whatever prize contender Valkyrie had just dropped on the Grandmaster's doorstep made her believe she'd just assumed the advantage.

"You paid her twice? I've brought you far better specimens. This one looks homeless, dragged from a gutter," Topaz protested. The Grandmaster held up his hand to calm her.

"And I'm sure you will again, my dear. You know you're still my favorite. But if Scrapper 142 says there's something special about this one—"

"I can hear you. And I assure you, I'm far from a gutter-dweller." Thor rose to his full height. He walked toward the Grandmaster but was suddenly zapped again and yelped in pain. The Grandmaster held up a fob control identical to Valkyrie's.

"Just a precaution. I know the Obedience Disks can be a nuisance," he said. "But necessary in most cases.

Although I haven't ever been very fond of the name. It was a working title while we were in the testing phase, and no one seemed to put 'Find better name' on the agenda, so it stuck."

Thor struggled through the agony and stood up once again, gritting his teeth in determination, refusing to show signs of pain on his face.

"Well, well. You are a contender, aren't you? Tell me, what's your story? Who are you, where do you come from?" The Grandmaster sat back, genuine interest clearly in his eyes.

"I am Thor Odinson, from Asgard. The god of thunder." Thor squared his shoulders proudly.

" 'God of thunder'? That sounds promising." The Grandmaster looked around the room, and his guests all nodded in agreement. "Really, I have to see this. Show me the thunder, Thor of Asgard."

Thor gave a defiant look, raised his hand high, and closed his eyes. Sparks of electricity began to collect around his hand, but quickly sputtered out and dissipated.

Thor looked at his hand, confused. "It . . . it works better with my hammer."

"How many times have we heard that, right?" the

Grandmaster asked the room, chuckling. "Still, I think with a little snip here and a polish there, I can sell you to the audience."

"What is this audience you speak of?" Thor demanded.

"Oh, just a little thing I like to call the Contest of Champions, the greatest event in the galaxy. And I am the Grandmaster, the highly adored host of the arena and all things on Sakaar. Strange you've never heard of the Contest, though." The Grandmaster seemed slightly baffled and mildly offended.

"I've been...busy," Thor replied, trying not to insult the Grandmaster and risk getting shocked again.

"Well, in any case, two contenders enter the arena; only one exits: the Champion. If you win, you may ask for any wish you desire." The Grandmaster had a gleam in his eyes. "Right now we're at our highest attendance ever, thanks to our current Champion. He's unbeatable. Truly magnificent. You have to meet him." The Grandmaster laughed. "What am I saying—of course you'll meet him, just before he probably squashes you. Then again, I don't know how easy Asgardians are to squash. Let me ask... ah, there he is."

The Grandmaster pointed a finger, and the crowd of

Sakaarian elites parted to reveal...Loki? The Trickster gave a smug look at his brother as he approached.

"Brother? How—?" Thor was thoroughly perplexed at the sight of Loki.

"The same as you, I would gather. Although I do seem to appear to have found myself a 'contender' as well. One more in keeping with my own set of skills."

"Brother?" the Grandmaster crowed. "Why, how wonderful! Here I am, reuniting families without even realizing it." His cronies all nodded appreciatively at the Grandmaster's unintended kindness.

"You must free me," Thor said urgently to Loki in a low voice. "Convince this Grandmaster to let me go, then come back with me to Asgard. There is a terrible darkness spreading...." But Thor's pleas fell on deaf ears.

"Back to Asgard? Where no one really ever appreciated me for who I really am? I'd rather not, thank you. Especially if there's some 'darkness' overtaking the land." Loki sat on a couch near Thor. "I believe I've finally found my place."

"Your place is with your people," Thor snapped.

Loki grinned, waving an arm across the room. "Exactly. Now, if you want to go back to Asgard, I suggest you work your way home. Go after that wish, and you just might earn it."

The Grandmaster's ears perked up. "Earning the wish? Well, you'll have to enter the arena as soon as possible, won't you?"

"I'm ready," Thor declared.

The Grandmaster looked him up and down. "*Mmmm*, not yet. Topaz, will you kindly escort our contender to his new home?"

With a look of disdain, Topaz took out an Obedience Disk controller, turned Thor around, and escorted him out of the Grandmaster's chamber, zapping Thor at various intervals.

Thor groaned as his body once again convulsed in the waves of electric shocks. He suddenly had a feeling that the journey home was going to be far more difficult than he had imagined.

Several moments later, Thor was unceremoniously thrown by an unsmiling Topaz into a dark room in a cavern that ran beneath the surface of Sakaar. The entrance was then sealed by electric bars. Thor looked around, seeing more cells like his lining the tunnels.

"Don't even think of trying to escape," came a voice from the back of his cell. Thor jumped slightly, not realizing he was sharing his jail cell with another prisoner. He peered in the back corner, and a humanoid pile of rocks nearly seven feet tall stood and walked toward him.

"You're Kronan, are you not?" Thor had encountered members of his cellmate's race before.

"Korg. And you're Asgardian. I've heard of you." Korg seemed a quiet soul for such a large presence.

"Are you here to face this 'Champion' as well?" Thor asked.

Korg shook his head. "I was captured during a revolt against the bounty hunters the Grandmaster sends out for the Contest. I had seen many of my kind taken, never to return. When I arrived, I found out why."

"You don't want this wish he's offering? You could end the suffering of your kind."

Korg again shook his large head. "I like to live. And as long as I stay here, no other Kronan lives will be taken. So I stick to the undercard, the warm-up before the main event." Korg settled himself back in his corner. "If you're smart, you'll do the same."

Thor steeled his eyes. "I aim to defeat the Champion and earn my way home."

"The only way to do that is to kill him, and that thing is unstoppable. I don't think it *can* be killed."

Thor turned to face Korg, ready for whatever the Grandmaster could throw at him. "Unkillable?" Thor scoffed. "He clearly has yet to meet me."

CHAPTER

Thor spent the entire night awake, unable to think of anything besides facing the Grandmaster's Champion. Around midday, he and a small band of prisoners were escorted into a large staging area adjacent to the arena. Weapons and armor of all shapes and sizes lined the walls for the would-be fighters to arm themselves with in the coming battles.

As Thor took in his surroundings, he caught sight of a familiar figure. "Valkyrie!" he cried out. Valkyrie turned toward him, another newly acquired prisoner in tow. "Speak with the Grandmaster. Free me and return to save our homeland. For Asgard!"

Valkyrie raised an eyebrow. "You're on Sakaar, not

Asgard. Save your pleas for the arena. Not that it'll help much." She turned and started walking away. "Asgard shouldn't hold its breath waiting for your return. You'll be dead soon," she said bluntly, calling over her shoulder.

Thor rolled his eyes at her departure. Not exactly the warm-and-fuzzy type, then.

As she disappeared around a corner, a loud cheer could be heard coming from the direction of the arena. A moment later Korg came lumbering down the ramp, shield dented, but he was otherwise unharmed.

"You won, I see," Thor said, impressed.

"It's why I stay, like I said," Korg replied. He paused in front of Thor for a moment, and his eyes grew soft. "I'm sorry for what's about to come. If it means anything, I think you deserve better. Good luck, friend."

Before Thor could reply, a squat alien with an apron made his way to Thor. He looked the Asgardian over a few times, gave a satisfied grunt, and pulled out a razor. Thor raised a fist in opposition, but two guards held him back.

The squat alien motioned to a chair in the corner. "Let's get you ready to fight now."

Without much choice in the matter, Thor sat but looked on defiantly. "I'm always ready to fight."

The immense octagonal arena was filled to capacity for the day's fight. Hundreds of thousands of spectators, creatures and races that spanned the galaxy, crowded next to one another, their excitement palpable. Above them, ships of all shapes hovered to view the events below. There was never a dull moment in the Grandmaster's Contests, but today the crowd both above and below felt something especially glorious was about to happen. Their beloved Champion was set to fight, and from what everyone heard, this would be a matchup for the ages.

The VIP suite had the perfect vantage point, and lavish couches and chairs lined the section. A long couch stretched almost its entire length. Seated there was the Grandmaster himself. He motioned to Loki, who was mingling among the other guests farther inside the suite, indicating the Asgardian should sit near him.

"Shall we start this?" The Grandmaster was grinning from ear to ear, rubbing his hands together.

Loki could barely contain his enthusiasm. Finally his arrogant brother would be brought to heel. "To say I've dreamt of a moment like this would be a gross understatement."

"Excellent. Let's give the people what they want, then."

In the center of the arena, a sixty-foot-tall projection of the Grandmaster suddenly appeared, arms outstretched. "People of Sakaar, travelers, lovers of great sport: Welcome to the Contest of Champions, the greatest show in the galaxy!" The crowd roared in excitement. "It's main event time, and do I have a show for you. First, your challenger." The audience was mixed with both cheers and boos.

The Grandmaster motioned for silence. "Now, now, let's show some sportsmanship. Hailing all the way from Asgard, I present the self-proclaimed god of thunder, Thor!"

Thor emerged from the shadows, battle ready. His hair was cut close to the scalp, his beard trimmed. He wore armor that resembled that of his Asgardian suit. Sheathed on his back were two swords, with a well-worn shield strapped to one arm, and a large mace in his other hand. He kicked at the floor, testing its density and the sand on it. There was no give, so any fall could—would—be brutal.

The crowd erupted at the sight of him. In the seats, people were placing bets on how long this newcomer would last. Thor looked around, trying to take in the enormity of his surroundings.

"And the legend that requires no introduction," the Grandmaster continued as the doors across the arena began to open slowly. Thor swore he could already hear the creature's breathing through the din of the audience. He placed a helmet on his head and assumed a fighting stance, facing the doors.

The Grandmaster's projected image gestured toward the opening door. "Your undefeated Champion, the wonder you all come back for time and again, to see him smash his foes. The one, the only *Incredible*—"

An enormous roar split the air, cutting off the Grandmaster's introduction. Without waiting for the doors to open completely, a behemoth exploded through the gate, demolishing the entrance. The gigantic figure was nearly ten feet of solid muscle. He wore a Spartan-like helmet, armor covering one shoulder, a battle-axe gripped tightly in one hand and a large war hammer in the other.

And he was green. Oh-so very green.

The audience rose as one to their feet, a deafening cheer filling the arena. The Champion let out a cry that seemed to overwhelm that of the crowd's as he beat his war hammer into the ground. The Grandmaster's projection vanished. Back in his suite, he turned to Loki and smiled.

"A beauty, isn't he?" the Grandmaster asked Loki.

For his part, Loki was trying to sink as far down into the lush couch as possible. His face paled. This Champion was no stranger to him. He nodded weakly to the Grandmaster in agreement.

In the arena, Thor took in the sight of the Champion and felt the last thing he expected: hope. The figure before him was equally familiar, but unlike Loki, this was a friend. In fact, he would know the creature anywhere, no matter the setting or attire. Before him, the Champion was none other than *the Hulk*!

Thor raised his mace and let out a shout of excitement. The audience quieted, clearly caught off guard by Thor's reaction. The Grandmaster looked at Thor quizzically as well.

"We know each other!" Thor looked up to the Grandmaster's suite, a broad smile crossing his face. "He's a friend from work!" He turned back to face the Hulk. "Banner, come, let us team up and—"

The Hulk let out another roar at the sound of his alter ego's name. He pawed the ground like a steed readying itself to charge. He exhaled loudly. Thor began to realize with a heightening sense of dread that there was no look of familiarity in his fellow Avenger's eyes, only a blood-lust. Still, he pushed on, confident there must just be some sort of misunderstanding.

"We needn't fight, Banner. You know me, remember?" Thor's arms were outstretched in a calming manner, but the gesture was lost on the Hulk.

"No Banner. Only Hulk!" he bellowed.

Without warning, the Hulk quickly stomped across the arena toward Thor. Thor nimbly flipped over the rampaging beast's back. The Hulk stopped and turned.

"I guess reasoning is out of the question here," Thor muttered to himself. He began to twirl his mace as the Hulk readied himself for another charge. As the green Goliath bounded toward him, Thor hurled his mace directly at the Hulk's face. The Hulk swatted it away and raised a fist. Thor dodged to the side, barely avoiding being pummeled into the ground.

Thor pulled the two swords from their sheaths on his back and prepared for the Hulk's next onslaught. Lifting his war hammer high, the Hulk swung the weapon down. Thor blocked it with the two swords. A loud *clank* echoed in the arena and the swords broke in two, but Thor was saved. The crowd gasped as one.

The Grandmaster turned to Loki. "Your Asgardian comrade is quite impressive, I have to admit."

"He certainly likes to think of himself as such," Loki said, rolling his eyes.

The Hulk began twirling his battle-axe and war hammer in an intricate and deadly pattern. Thor tossed aside the now-broken swords and backed away, watching and searching for an opening. This time, he swiftly lunged at the oncoming Hulk and stopped the war hammer with his shield. The weapon flew out of the Hulk's hand. A punch to the arm caused the Hulk to drop his axe. Thor kicked his enraged opponent away, and the two rolled to opposite ends of the arena.

"Hulk! We are friends!" Thor called out across the arena. "We need not entertain this any longer!"

The crowd booed Thor's attempt to cease the Contest and began to chant *"Champion!"* over and over. The Hulk lowered his head, preparing to dash. Thor crouched in a runner's stance, ready to meet in the middle.

The two friends-turned-opponents sprinted toward each other. Just as they reached the middle, the Hulk leaped up, both fists raised high. Thor, anticipating this approach, timed his jump so he was just under the Hulk as he jumped off the ground. A powerful uppercut from Thor connected with the Hulk's jaw, and the crowd gasped as the blow knocked the helmet off their Champion's head.

With the Hulk caught off guard, Thor began to land blow after blow on his big, green head. The Hulk began to swing wildly, missing each time as every punch thrown by Thor landed, knocking the Champion more and more off balance. Thor could feel the Hulk weakening, and even as he wanted to stop and force the Hulk to recognize him as his friend, not his adversary, Thor knew he had to keep going so he could win the Contest and get his wish, and get home to Asgard.

Suddenly, a jolt of electricity shot through Thor. He fell to the ground, writhing in pain, his stride broken. Looking toward the Grandmaster's suite, he saw the man hold up a control in one hand as he waved his finger back and forth.

It was the Obedience Disk.

Seizing upon Thor's moment of weakness, the Hulk grabbed the Asgardian by his feet and began to swing him back and forth, slamming Thor into the ground left and right and left and right. Loki, having been on the receiving end of this move before, stifled a grin in the VIP suite.

Thor lay on the ground of the arena, bloodied and bruised. He watched in paralyzed pain as the Hulk launched himself in the air, nearly as high as the ships hovering above. The brute began his descent, fists-first. At the last possible second, Thor rolled away, a hair-breadth from being smashed to a probable death.

"Hulk," Thor gasped. "Banner, remember who you are. We are friends."

The Hulk paused for a moment. "Friends?"

The Grandmaster stood with the rest of the audience, clapping, cheering for his Champion to deliver the final blow. But the Hulk looked at Thor, lying helpless in the sand at his feet.

"Yes...friends. Hulk and Thor." The Asgardian begged the fates for his words to get through to the Hulk.

The Hulk reached down and grabbed Thor by the chest.

"Friend," he whispered into Thor's ear, right before he hurled Thor back down one final time, and the last thing Thor saw was the floor of the arena rising up to meet him just before everything went black.

CHAPTER

The dull roar in his ears certainly wasn't the audience—that much Thor knew. How long he had been out was a different question entirely. As was the question of where he currently was. As he drifted in and out of consciousness, his eyes began to take in the room around him. He was laid out on a soft leather sofa built for someone of a much greater size than he. There was thick-looking carpeting lining the floors, and lush red velvet curtains that blocked out any light that might try to filter through. A massive four-poster bed sat in one corner of the room. As the roaring in his head died down, Thor thought he could hear bubbles. Maybe he was suffering from a concussion.

But then, turning his head, Thor witnessed a sight he never thought he would behold: the Hulk lounging in a natural hot spring as though it were a hot tub, emitting a moan of deep and appreciative pleasure as the soothing water relaxed his battle-weary muscles.

"Where am I?" Thor asked.

"Hulk home. Thor friend. Friend rest." The Hulk rattled off the statements as facts, no room to argue. Not that Thor would. He knew how close he came to dying in that arena. The Grandmaster's meddling nearly cost Thor his life. Fortunately, Thor realized he had been able to get through to his friend. The Hulk had somehow managed to save Thor from total obliteration, and that meant some semblance of Banner clung to this gargantuan, battling Champion. Thor felt the small spark of hope flare once again.

"Hulk. Thank you for sparing me. We are alone, yes?" The Hulk nodded. "May I speak with Banner?"

The Hulk stirred in the spring, his brow furrowing. "No Banner, only Hulk."

His tone told Thor not to push the matter at the moment. "Very well. Good to know. How did you get here? How long have you been on this planet, Hulk?"

The look on the Hulk's face changed to one of confusion. "Hulk not know. A ship, then Hulk here. Hulk fight. Hulk win."

Thor's heart sank. The ship must have been the Quinjet, on which Banner had left after the Battle of Sokovia. He'd turned off his comm, and that was the last the Avengers had heard of him . . . until now. Had his friend been here all these years since?

"Hulk . . . we tried tracking you, all of us, to bring you home," Thor began carefully.

But the Hulk ignored him, standing up and splashing water everywhere as he climbed out of the spring, dried, and began to dress for battle. A newly repaired helmet hung alongside a wall of weapons.

"Hulk home now." He sounded resigned to the fact and even happy about it, or as happy as the Hulk could get.

"It doesn't have to be. We can leave here. Together! Please, Hulk, my home—Asgard—it . . . it needs me. Now more than ever. And with your strength, I could really use you there with me."

The Hulk had finished dressing. "Hulk home. Thor friend. Thor stay."

Thor warily got to his feet. "Hulk, please. At least

release me. Convince the Grandmaster to set me free so I can leave and—"

Thor suddenly found himself face-to-face with the Hulk, his large eyes narrowed. "Thor friend. Thor stay."

The tiniest of taps from the Hulk put Thor back on the oversize sofa.

As the Hulk began to exit his chamber, Thor gave a weak wave. "Stay alive. Although you seem to be doing a fairly good job of that," he muttered as his friend and savior left.

Thor waited until he could hear the uproarious cheering of the crowd far in the distance as their Champion reentered the arena. Thor creeped to the door and looked around. The coast was clear. He went to the wall and chose a nasty-looking spiked ball and chain, and headed toward the exit. As soon as he passed completely through it, however, his body was hit with a massive jolt of electricity that sent him reeling. He tried to walk forward, but the pain from the Obedience Disk was too much, and he collapsed, falling back into the Hulk's suite.

"Plan...B?" Thor wondered aloud as he fell to the ground, losing consciousness once again.

He came to a little while later, finding himself back on the luxurious sofa. Thor saw the Hulk pacing the room. "Congratulations, I assume?" Thor asked mildly.

Hearing his friend awake, the Hulk marched over to Thor and pointed at the Obedience Disk. "Thor friend. Friend stay!"

"Yes, yes, I know. 'Hulk home,' doesn't want to leave. We've tried that route." Thor's mind raced. He knew there had to be a way out. Looking toward the door, he smiled. *Of course*, he thought. *The way out is quite often the way in.* An idea quickly formed.

"Hulk, Thor friend, yes?" The Hulk nodded. "What if I told you I had a friend here, someone I would very much like to see? Could you get them for me? As a favor?"

"Thor stay?" The Hulk sounded hesitant.

Thor nodded. "Yes, Thor stay. Right here until you return."

With that, Thor began to tell the Hulk who he needed to see and how to find them.

"You *must* be kidding me with this."

Thor turned at the sound of the voice coming from the

entrance. It was Valkyrie! The Hulk walked past her and plopped himself on the large sofa.

"Thor friend," he said to Valkyrie by way of explanation.

"Not one of mine," she answered, and turned to leave.

"Wait!" Thor cried out. "Before I fell off the Bifrost, in the darkness that was consuming it, I feel like I may have seen something...a woman. She has been plaguing my nightmares, and now I fear she has Asgard in her grasp."

Valkyrie stopped at Thor's revelation. She shook her head as she turned. "Where is Odin? Shouldn't he be protecting his kingdom?"

"He...I don't know. He's not on Asgard, though." Thor moved toward her, taking hold of her arm. "You know something, don't you?"

"That you don't know, or haven't figured it out, shows how much Odin has prepared his heir. And what little he cares of the other Valkyries after..." Her voice trailed off.

"What? After what? Tell me so I can fix whatever it is my father has failed to."

Valkyrie's eyes flashed in anger. "That was our job! Odin tasked the Valkyries to drive back what has returned."

"And that is?" Thor was anxious. The answer was so near.

"Hela." Valkyrie spat out the name of Old Asgard's ancient enemy. "Goddess of the dead, ruler of Hel. We fought hard to drive her back, and a curse was placed on her: As long as Odin sits on the throne, Asgard would be safe from her."

Thor's head fell. "And because of my brother's manipulations, Odin was dethroned and has been wandering Midgard for some time."

"Giving Hela the time and opportunity she needed. To raise an attack." She patted Thor on the shoulder. "Sorry, but Asgard's doomed, and there's nothing you can do about it."

Thor's eyes lit up. "There is a way off this world. I know how. I just don't know where. The vessel that brought my friend here, do you know where it is?"

Valkyrie shrugged. "Probably in the old shipyard near the marketplace. Not that it'll do you any good. It's not like you're going anywhere."

Thor suddenly grinned and squeezed Valkyrie in a tight hug, prompting a sound of disgust from her as she pushed him away and stomped toward the door. He walked after her. The Hulk had nodded off during their conversation, and Thor gave a silent wave to his sleeping friend as he walked through the doorway, unharmed.

Valkyrie was stunned. "How—?"

Thor held up the Obedience Disk controller, which he had lifted off her when he'd given her a hug. He'd used the controller to disable the Obedience Disk on his chest, which no longer glowed. He reached for it and popped it off his chest, slipping it into his belt. With that, he turned and raced out of the suite, leaving a speechless Valkyrie and a snoring Hulk behind.

CHAPTER

The shipyard looked like the galaxy's version of a used car lot. Ships of all sizes and conditions were piled two or three deep, some on top of others, rusting away. Thor darted in and out of the rows until...

There!

He ran to a familiar-looking ship. It was slightly dusty but looked to be in one piece. "I could kiss you," he happily told the Quinjet, the same ship that had brought the Hulk to the planet.

He climbed into the cockpit and searched for the controls to turn it on. A voice suddenly came from the speakers. "Please speak the activation code."

"Yes!" Thor exclaimed. "*Ummm*, let's try: Avengers, assemble."

"I'm sorry, that is incorrect," the ship replied.

Thor racked his brain. What would Tony Stark have programmed into this? Sighing, he tried again. "Tony Stark is a genius."

The Quinjet's control board lit up. "Activation code accepted."

Thor laughed at his good fortune. He reached to fire up the engines when suddenly he heard a *RIIIIIIP* from the back of the ship. Turning, he saw that the Hulk had followed him to the shipyard and was now in the process of tearing off the back end of the Quinjet.

"Thor friend. Thor stay!" the Hulk roared at him.

Before Thor could respond, the Quinjet, lights flickering, spoke once more. "Voice recognition. Bruce Banner, Hulk. Message retrieval activated."

Thor looked at the controls as a familiar face appeared on the screen: It was Natasha Romanoff, also known as Black Widow. She and the Hulk had been close friends back when the Hulk was still on Earth, fighting alongside the Avengers.

"Hey, big guy," she began haltingly, her features sad and worried. "Not sure if you're out there. Not sure if you're even getting these. Fifth I've sent so far. I know you must be scared out there, wherever you are. But everything will be fine." The screen flickered for a moment and Black Widow reappeared. "I miss you. And the sun's getting real low...."

The image faded as the message ended. Thor turned. The Hulk's gaze was transfixed on the screen. He reached out to touch it, and as he did so, his arm began to shrink, along with his entire body.

Slowly, the Hulk transformed back into Bruce Banner.

Thor raced to embrace his friend. "She encoded a trigger phrase! Brilliant work! I wish I knew about that one. It would have saved a beating and a lot of hurt. But welcome back!"

Bruce was in a state of shock. He pushed out of Thor's friendly embrace and looked around wildly. "Where—where am I?" Memories began to come racing back, and he started to panic. "Ultron! Sokovia! We have to stop him. I didn't want to harm anyone else. I wanted to—"

Thor tried to calm Banner. "My friend, please. Listen to me. Ultron was defeated. The Avengers destroyed him."

"When? How?" Banner was baffled.

"Two years ago." Thor sighed, hating to deliver the news.

Banner's eyes widened. "Two—two *years*?" Looking around, he took in the alien sights and sounds. Turning to Thor, a terrified look crossed his features. "Hulk. He's been in control this whole time. Do I even want to know what he's been doing?"

"Probably best you don't. Let's just say you're quite popular here, and very recognizable, so try and remain calm and in control."

"Says the god of thunder." Banner's voice was tinged with panic as he tried to breathe.

"Not so much on *this* world."

Banner looked at Thor, desperation in his eyes. "So, what's the plan? How do we get out of here and back home?"

Thor nodded to the Quinjet, which was now torn in two. "Well, our first option is off the table. But I know someone who might be able to help."

"You've lost them *both*? The blond one I can kind of understand, but the Champion, too? How do you lose a two-ton green killing monster?!"

Valkyrie winced as the Grandmaster's tirade continued. The Grandmaster, for his part, tried to calm himself as he paced his chamber. "Think, think, think. Ah! A game!"

"Game?" Valkyrie raised an eyebrow. Now did not seem the time for games.

"A contest. See who can find them first. You or"—he turned to face Loki, who was seated comfortably in the corner—"his brother."

Loki appeared taken aback. "Me? Whatever reason for? Games are my forte, but not these sorts. Mine are more...cerebral, shall we say?"

"You are related. You know how he thinks. And..." The Grandmaster paused, a gleam in his eye. "You love money."

This piqued both Valkyrie's and Loki's interests. "How much are we talking?" Valkyrie asked.

"More than you've ever been paid. Combined." The Grandmaster's face turned serious. "The first of you to find my Champion and return him to me wins. As for the Asgardian, do whatever you want with him. He's too much trouble as it is."

Valkyrie and Loki eyed each other, sizing up their

new competition. "What are you waiting for? Go!" the Grandmaster ordered. With that, the contest was on between the two new rivals.

⚡🔨⚡

"This is insane. You know that, right?" Banner was racing to keep up with Thor. He was wearing new clothes found in an emergency compartment in the Quinjet: jeans and a T-shirt that read STARK RULES.

"The situation is a bit dire—I'll give you that," Thor replied.

"I meant all of this." Bruce gestured widely to emphasize his point.

The two were racing through the streets of the marketplace. Everywhere, there were vendors selling Champion merchandise. Hulk masks, shirts, fists that roared when punched together.

"I told you; he's quite popular here." Thor led them out of the market and accidentally straight into a parade celebrating the Champion. A band was playing, and green powder exploded everywhere.

One parade-goer pointed what looked like a party favor at Bruce's face and pulled a string, and—POP!—Bruce was covered in the green powder.

Bruce could feel himself starting to lose control in the face of all this Hulk-mania. He fought for calm. "The sun's getting real low.... The sun's getting real low," Bruce repeated as he stumbled through the crowd, blinded by the powder. He crashed into a rather unpleasant-looking alien, who immediately took offense. Bruce looked around, but he had lost Thor in the crowd. The angered alien began to raise his fist, ready to pummel Bruce when...*ZZZZZZAP!* He began to shake uncontrollably and fell facedown.

Bruce examined the alien and saw an Obedience Disk attached to his back. "You're new," came a voice from behind him.

Bruce turned and saw Valkyrie. She was holding the controller for the Obedience Disk in her hand as she looked him over. "Too bad you're of no use to me. You wouldn't last five seconds in the arena."

"You have no idea how wrong you are," Thor said, pushing his way to them.

"Arena? What arena?" Bruce's confusion was compounded the longer he stayed.

"Valkyrie, meet your Champion." Thor motioned toward the baffled Bruce.

Valkyrie looked stunned at the sight of the once-unstoppable force of nature reduced to this human standing before her. "This? But he's so"—she wrinkled her nose—"puny."

Banner stood a little taller, taking offense. "I prefer the term *academic*."

Thor moved to Valkyrie. "I've been searching for you."

"I was about to say the same thing," she replied.

"Please. Tell me you're here to help." Thor's face grew hopeful.

Valkyrie scoffed and motioned for the pair to follow her. She shook her head. "You're persistent, I'll give you that. Thickheaded, but persistent."

CHAPTER

10

The trio made their way through the parade, dodging and weaving around overly enthusiastic partyers all celebrating the Hulk's triumphs. Bruce still couldn't believe there was a place where his destructive alter ego could be so beloved.

"So, how do you two know each other?" he yelled to Valkyrie and Thor above the din of the revelers.

"She is a great warrior of Asgard lore," Thor said.

"He was my prisoner," Valkyrie said at the same time. "I brought him to fight you."

Banner was taken aback. "We...fought?" His eyes grew wide with dread. "Did I hurt you?"

Thor waved away his friend's concerns. "Nothing time

and maybe some healing waters and fine wine in Asgard can't cure."

Valkyrie smiled at the notion that Bruce was unaware of his actions as the Hulk. "He's lucky you two are friends," she told him. "You've been the Champion for a while for a reason."

Banner seemed despondent. "This celebration, these people, they adore the Hulk. What did I do to deserve this?"

"Well, you managed to successfully ki—"

Thor interrupted Valkyrie, desperate to change the subject. "Where are we going?"

"My ship. The Grandmaster wants you, and I'm turning down a lot of money for doing this, so I *might* change my mind." Valkyrie's tone had altered since they'd last spoken, Thor noticed.

"Why the change of heart?" Thor was genuinely curious.

A sigh came from Valkyrie. "Hela. You had to go and tell me she was back." The warrior shook her head. "It is a Valkyrie's duty to protect Asgard from her. When she attacked before, I was too young and naive to think I could handle her on my own." She paused, remembering her past. "I didn't last beyond the first wave of her attack."

"So you'll return with me to Asgard and finish what

you started?" Thor was pleased he had finally gotten through to her.

"I'll do what I can to get you to Asgard. *Then* we'll see what I do." Valkyrie motioned for them to follow her. "We're here."

Thor recognized the sleek vessel from earlier, when she'd captured him to deliver him to the Grandmaster. Valkyrie's ship was clearly one of the finer ships flying the Sakaarian skies. The three got on board.

"You'll need to sit up here with me. We have company in the back." Valkyrie turned their attention to a bound and gagged figure in the rear of the ship. It was Loki. Thor immediately grabbed the nearest object, a wrench, and threw it at his brother. The wrench hit Loki squarely in the chest, and he let out a muffled cry.

"I had to be sure," Thor explained. "He's known for his illusions."

"*I* had to be sure he wouldn't beat me in the Grand-master's bet in case he found you first and took you to the crazy fool, like the lapdog he's become." Valkyrie clearly had no patience for the Trickster.

Thor chuckled. "You've come to know my brother well."

"Loki's here? Are you guys insane? Don't you remember

what he did to us all the last time?" Bruce was warily eye-ing the tied-up villain.

"Yes, and I'm sure he remembers who it was that helped put an end to his mad quest. If he moves, feel free to go green on him again." Thor smiled as Loki visibly paled at the memory.

Valkyrie was punching coordinates into her navigation system. "I figure our best bet is to get to Xandar, refuel, and stock up on supplies. If we maintain top speed, we should reach Asgard in eighteen months or so."

Thor was aghast. *"Eighteen months?* Asgard may not even have eighteen hours if Hela has truly returned and is as deadly as you say!"

"I'm the one with the ship, but I'm open to sugges-tions." Valkyrie sat back, confident that hers was the best option.

"Is there a faster ship?" Thor asked. Valkyrie shook her head. He scanned the sky, looking at the many worm-holes. "We came here through one of those. Perhaps we can return the same way."

Valkyrie laughed in his face. "Okay, Thunder God. Pick one and I'll tell you how that won't work."

He pointed at the vast wormhole that took up nearly a

third of the sky. "That one. It seems like it could lead us wherever we need to be in the shortest amount of time."

Slack-jawed, Valkyrie gazed at Thor in silence for a moment before bursting into a fit of hysterics. "You expect me to fly into the Magnetar? This ship wouldn't last a minute in there, and I didn't sign up for a suicide run."

Banner pushed his way into the cockpit to get a better view. "You have a Magnetar wormhole here?"

"You know of this?" Thor asked.

"I studied it as part of my fourth doctorate."

"Then you can help us navigate through it. Perfect!" Thor beamed.

Bruce didn't look as convinced. "I don't think you understand. The interior of a Magnetar wormhole is such that even a teaspoon of its atmosphere would have the mass of a hundred million tons."

Thor looked at his friend, not grasping the issue. "*Sooooo...*"

"We drink and toast to an impossible plan," Valkyrie answered.

"Surely there is a way, Banner." Thor was insistent.

Bruce thought for a moment. "Well, assuming none of us black out from the pressure during the journey, then we would still need a ship that could withstand the geodetic strain of the wormhole without shields, *and* some kind of off-line power-steering mechanism that could function without the onboard computer system."

Valkyrie stared at Bruce. "You're right. *Academic* suits you better than *puny*."

"Can we find such a vessel here?" Thor asked.

A series of muffled grunts and sounds came from the back. They turned to see Loki trying to spit out his gag. Thor cautiously approached his brother and took off the binding around his mouth.

"Finally. Thank you. If you had let me join the conversation earlier, I could have avoided Doctor Banner's physics lesson." Thor moved to replace the gag, but Loki dodged him. "Apologies. One tends to get a bit testy when tied up in the back of a strange ship and having tools tossed at him."

"You said you had a solution? Spit it out." Thor's patience was wearing thin.

"The Grandmaster gave me a tour of his palace, and he has a collection of only the finest ships in the galaxy in his garage."

"So we hot-wire a ship from the guy that's held me hostage for two years?" Bruce asked incredulously.

"Have you a better idea?" Loki retorted.

Bruce shook his head. "Just making sure we were screwing over the right guy."

Loki turned back to Thor. "Free me, brother, and I can lead you to where he stores his ships. I have studied his compound and am certain we can easily evade detection and find the ship we need." Loki looked and sounded sincere. Thor paused for a moment before unbinding his brother.

The unlikely pair began to exit the ship before Thor stopped, looking back to Valkyrie. "For this to work, I think it best if we have some sort of distraction."

A grin crossed Valkyrie's face. "I think I know just the thing."

As Loki and Thor exited the ship, Valkyrie lifted off and headed toward the arena.

Thor looked at his brother. "We'll only have one chance at this. Do not mess it up."

Loki smiled. "Trust me, brother. I have everything under control."

Bruce watched as Valkyrie landed her ship in the middle of the arena. "What are you planning?"

"If I were you, I'd worry less about that and more

about staying small and pink." Valkyrie smiled. "Everyone out there might love the Champion, but these guys may not be so happy to see Big Green. You're their main competition."

Banner waited in the ship as Valkyrie easily took out two guards stationed in front of a dark cavern. Within moments, he began to hear an approaching roar and felt the ground shake. Valkyrie came bolting out of the entrance to the cavern. Bruce couldn't believe his eyes when he saw what followed her.

Dozens of aliens came pouring out of the cavern. Weapons were being passed around to each as the freed prisoners armed themselves. Valkyrie's ship began its ascent, and she and Bruce flew over Korg, who had taken control of the freed prisoners and was readying the group for battle.

Valkyrie flipped a switch, and a loudspeaker projected her voice to the crowd below. Looking at Korg, she said, "The god of thunder sends his best."

With that, she flew off as a full-scale riot began.

CHAPTER

Can anyone please explain to me how things got to this point?" the Grandmaster demanded as he made his way through the corridors of his massive ship. Looking onto the dismal scene below, he saw his finest fighters, who he had been grooming for his beloved Contests, inciting a riot, running through the streets, destroying anything that bore the Champion's face.

A guard approached the Grandmaster. "Well, sir, the slaves—"

The Grandmaster cut him off with a glare. "What have I said about that word?"

The guard, chagrined, corrected himself. "The 'prisoners with jobs' were freed, it appears, by Scrapper 142."

Topaz snorted from behind the Grandmaster. "Figures. I told you she couldn't be trusted," she said smugly.

"Now, now. This is not the time for petty jealousies. We need constructive criticism. And a plan. An extra week's pay for the person who comes up with the best plan. Go!" The Grandmaster settled himself in the plush captain's chair on the deck of the ship and watched as his city erupted in chaos. His ship was soon flanked by a half-dozen warships meant to end this riot—and quickly.

Below, Korg looked up to see the man who had pillaged his beloved city for sport. His chance for redemption, and to complete the uprising he'd once been a part of, was finally at hand. With a cry, he ordered his fellow freed fighters to direct their attacks toward the ship. The Grandmaster's vessel was suddenly bombarded with blasts, rocks, and anything the rioters could throw or fire at it.

Growing more agitated, the Grandmaster repeated wildly, "The plan? Anyone?!"

"What *is* your plan here, brother?" Thor whispered as the two Asgardians skulked quietly through the depths of the Grandmaster's palace.

"Patience, dear brother. First we must worry about the two guards blocking our path."

Acting in tandem, the sons of Odin disarmed the guards and knocked them unconscious with one fluid movement.

"You'll help us free Asgard from Hela's grip when we arrive? I can count on you?" Thor asked.

"Of course. After all, I'm sure you blame me for her resurgence. It's the least I can do." Loki appeared contrite. "Although, I am curious, why the sudden change of heart to become Odinson and assume the throne?"

"It is what is needed to defeat Hela. Therefore it is my duty," Thor said plainly. He let out a small sigh, his voice almost apologetic. "In the past I demanded the throne when I hadn't earned it, and then refused the throne when Asgard needed me most. You stole it. Twice."

"Yet *you* are always forgiven," Loki said, trying not to sneer.

"My point is that our self-centered conflict over Asgard has ruined our kingdom. We have been so focused on fighting for the top we've forgotten there's a middle and a bottom. If I'm to be king, then I want to be a custodian, not a conqueror."

"Why the sudden baring of your soul to me?" Loki asked.

Thor turned to his brother. "Because I want to change. I want to be better. And I think you can, too. Helping us escape has shown you can take strides toward that." He looked at Loki earnestly. "Make a fresh start, brother. It's time."

The Grandmaster was at his wit's end. Never had he thought a day like this would come. All he'd worked for was vanishing before his eyes. Talking into the communications center's microphone, his voice was broadcast to those below.

"If you force me to kill you, then I won't have anyone for next week's fight! Can't we reach some sort of compromise? You, Korg…talk some sense into this mob." The Grandmaster flopped back into his chair, hoping his words got through to the protesters.

Below, Korg picked up a vendor's cart full of Champion flags and hurled it at the Grandmaster's ship. The Grandmaster sighed heavily. "So much for reason." He turned to a soldier stationed at a weapons control center and gave him a wave.

The ship's turrets turned to aim below. Gas began to leak out as the Grandmaster unleashed a chemical into the air. Korg covered his face and urged everyone to take cover as the fighting began to escalate.

CHAPTER

12

The brothers finally reached the Grandmaster's hangar. Before them was a vast array of ships from across the galaxy. Dozens lined the walls. Thor began to examine each one.

"If I may," Loki spoke up, "the Grandmaster's personal limousine is quite remarkable. A thing of beauty, really. He showed me the city in it when I first arrived."

"I doubt a luxury vehicle is what Banner called for," Thor answered.

"A shame. I would love to have one for my own."

Thor sighed. "I'm sure you would, brother. Will you at least start looking for anything resembling Banner's description?"

Loki laughed. "I merely said I could possibly show you

where to find what you were looking for. I didn't actually grasp a word he was babbling about."

"No matter. I think this may be exactly what we need." Thor stopped in front of a ship unlike any he had ever seen. It was glorious. Sleek yet sturdy, clearly top-of-the-line technology. The cockpit had more controls than Thor had ever seen in his life, even more advanced than something Tony Stark could possibly design. Probably.

"Ah, the *Commodore*. You have excellent taste, brother. The Grandmaster bragged about this one, calling it his newest acquisition."

"It is our acquisition now. Come. Valkyrie must be ready for us."

Thor and Loki quickly boarded the swift ship as the noise of the riots grew louder in the distance.

"Here they come," Valkyrie said, her voice tinged with envy. "Loki wasn't kidding. The Grandmaster has some beauties when it comes to ships."

"Speaking of . . ." Bruce said, pointing. "Incoming."

"I saw that one five seconds ago. I was waiting for it to get in range." She blasted the oncoming warship while still looking at Bruce.

"Show-off." Bruce had to admit, he was rather impressed by her skills as a warrior and pilot.

The comm crackled on in the ship. "*Commodore* to Valkyrie, do you copy?"

"Listen to you. Thor steals one ship and suddenly he starts talking like a pilot." Valkyrie gave a slight grin of approval.

"In case you hadn't noticed, your little 'distraction' has turned into an all-out war," came Thor's voice over the comm.

Valkyrie sat back, satisfied, taking it all in. "I know. Isn't it great?"

"Not the words I'd choose, considering we have another war to fight. I'd rather we exit this one as soon as possible." Thor did not sound amused. "Banner, will this ship suffice to make it through your wormhole?"

"I wouldn't exactly claim it as mine, but it looks sturdy. I'll need a closer examination to determine exactly—"

Valkyrie cut off Bruce. "Thor, do you know how to open the bay doors?"

"I believe so, yes. Why?" he replied.

"Open them up." She turned to Bruce. "I wanna make sure we survive this insane gambit of yours. So you need

Thor, son of Odin and prince of Asgard, is far from home and looking for answers. He's had a vision of a mysterious darkness that has been growing—and will soon come to his realm.

Things in Asgard have been odd while Thor has been away. And when things are amiss, it's likely due to some sort of scheme from Thor's brother, Loki. This time is no exception.

Discovering Loki has magically confused and cast their father to Earth, Thor makes his trickster brother come with him to recover Odin. A small illusion provides their New York City disguises.

As they leave to return to Asgard...

...they're ambushed and thrown through a portal to another world. Thor finds himself on a planet called Sakaar.

He soon realizes that it's a dangerous place, even for an Asgardian who counts himself a member of the Avengers. He is set upon by creatures with an electric net.

Luckily for Thor—or perhaps not—he is spotted by Scrapper 142, also known as Valkyrie. She intervenes, fighting off the aliens, but makes no move to help Thor out of the net. Instead, she drags him away.

She takes him to the Grandmaster, who rules Sakaar and has set up what he calls his Contest of Champions, in which warriors fight in his arena for huge crowds.

Of course, Loki is already there and surprised but delighted to see his brother captured.

The Grandmaster and his attendants prepare Thor for the arena. If he can best the current undefeated Champion, the Grandmaster will set him free so he can return to Asgard and continue his quest.

This is going to be a tougher fight than Thor imagined. The Champion is none other than his fellow Avenger the Hulk! The Hulk has no interest in teaming up. He just wants to fight.

But Thor is able to get through to the Hulk's alter ego, the genius Bruce Banner. They're still good friends, and Bruce wants to help Thor get off Sakaar.

With the help of Banner—and a surprise turn from Valkyrie—Thor is able to find a ship. He's finally able to start making his way home.

But even if he does get there, he'll face the greatest challenge of his life—the ancient, evil Hela.

a better look? No time like the present." Valkyrie flipped the ship in midair and pushed a button on the control panel, and Bruce was suddenly ejected from the ship.

He let out a scream as he descended, trying desperately not to transform into the Hulk out of fear. At the last second, the *Commodore* was under him, doors open. Banner fell through them and somehow landed softly in a cushioned chair.

"Anti-grav stabilizing interior atmosphere. This *is* an impressive ship." He was pleased, both by the ship and that he'd survived his fall from Valkyrie's ship.

"Excellent. Now, can you please examine the rest for our safe passage?" Thor was beginning to lose patience.

As Bruce looked over the ship's schematics, Thor searched the skies for Valkyrie's ship. He watched as she dodged and weaved through the warships.

At last, Bruce gave a nod. "Seems like this should work. In theory."

"Good enough for me. Valkyrie, we are all clear. Prepare to board," Thor said through the comm.

"One sec. I have one last score to settle," Valkyrie replied.

Bruce looked to the back of the *Commodore* and saw Loki. "He's still with us?"

"On surprisingly good behavior. He's probably worried about our green friend reappearing and knocking him around again," Thor responded. He watched as Valkyrie aimed her ship directly at the Grandmaster's. "Insane woman. What is she thinking?"

As if to answer his question, Valkyrie's ship's booster engines fired, speeding up her ship for a direct collision course with the cockpit of the Grandmaster's. Thor watched in horror as Valkyrie's ship smashed into the Grandmaster's, causing a huge explosion.

"No!" Thor exclaimed. His face looked stricken. Why would she sacrifice herself after all this? What had she been thinking?

"Wait, look." Bruce pointed. A small figure was headed straight toward them, flipping in midair as it descended. As the figure approached them at rapid-fire speed, Thor heaved a sigh of relief. It was Valkyrie!

She landed on the *Commodore*'s surface, standing upright. "Room for one more?" she quipped.

Thor opened the door and Valkyrie boarded the ship. "Scoot over, Thunder God. We're going to need a real pilot."

Taking control of the ship's steering, Valkyrie smiled.

"Now, *this* is the kind of ship I was born to fly. Hold on, boys." She revved up the engines, increasing the speed to maximum velocity. Behind them, the remaining warships followed, firing on the vessel, but Valkyrie easily evaded them.

She pulled the controls toward her, and the ship angled up. It began to climb higher and higher into the atmosphere. The warships peeled off, not built for the higher altitude nor willing to follow the *Commodore*'s flight path.

After all, it was headed straight for the Magnetar.

As they grew closer, debris whipped around them at crushing speeds. Lightning crashed in front of the ship as massive storms brewed on all sides. But Valkyrie expertly avoided everything the Magnetar was throwing at them.

"Last chance to back out. Anyone? Maybe eject the mischief-maker back there?" Valkyrie suggested, her face serious.

"Where I go, he goes. He must face what he has brought upon our home," Thor replied.

"Buckle in, because this might not be pretty." Valkyrie stared at the heart of the wormhole.

Thor and Bruce locked eyes for a moment in mutual agreement before Thor turned his gaze forward, his face set for what was to come. "For the glory of Asgard." Valkyrie glanced over at him, and Thor met her look. She gave a simple nod. She was ready.

Thor stared into the wormhole and braced himself, both for the flight they were about to embark on to reach Asgard, and the battle they would surely face once they got there. He knew he was ready. Ready for Hela. Ready for the fight.

And, most important, ready for the throne.

He gave a small smile as Valkyrie engaged the thrusters to full speed, and the *Commodore* vanished into the wormhole.

Thor was finally going home.

THOR: RAGNAROK
A NEW STORY

BY STEVE BEHLING

PROLOGUE

BEFORE

THE BATTLE OF NEW YORK

An invading force of otherworldly Chitauri warriors had flooded the city. Destruction followed in their wake. There seemed to be no stopping them. That was what most people thought, including the World Security Council. In an effort to contain the invasion and end it before it could spread across the world, the World Security Council was ready to give the order: Nuke New York.

It's quite possible that the city, and the rest of the world, would have fallen to the Chitauri. But it wouldn't have been because of the World Security Council's attempt to blow New York City off the map. That never happened. No, the turning of the tide came down to a team of six individuals, known collectively as the Avengers.

Two of those individuals were at present riding atop a great Chitauri beast that careened through the concrete canyons of the city. Thor and the Hulk fought side by side, comrades-in-arms, delivering blow after blow to the oncoming Chitauri. The warriors flung themselves at the heroes in an effort to destroy them utterly.

Pity for them it didn't work.

The two Avengers fought together in silence. Thor hammered the Chitauri with his enchanted hammer, Mjolnir. The Hulk smashed the Chitauri with his non-enchanted, huge, very hard fists. Both did the job quite nicely.

They didn't know what damage the Chitauri beast could cause if it escaped their grasp, and they didn't want to find out. The Hulk pried a hunk of the creature's metal hide from its body, heaved it over his head, and hurled it straight down. Seeing this, Thor turned his attention from the Chitauri warriors and drove his hammer into the hole that the Hulk had made. But he wasn't just striking the beast. Alone, the blow that Thor delivered would not have stopped the alien.

No. It was Mjolnir summoning lightning from the sky that delivered a terminal jolt to the massive monster.

An unearthly sound erupted from deep within the creature as it lost all control. One moment it had been soaring above the streets of Manhattan. The next it was headed straight on a collision course for the famed Grand Central

Terminal. The beast smashed through solid concrete, stone, metal, and glass, shattering the station to pieces, until it came screeching to a halt in the middle of the now-empty commuter hub.

The Hulk and Thor held on, riding the Chitauri beast to the ground.

They were victorious.

Each took a brief moment to catch his breath as debris from Grand Central Terminal piled around them. Thor surveyed the felled beast, satisfied that the two Avengers had done their job. He nodded slightly, as if to say, *We have fought well, my friend.*

The Hulk punched Thor in the head.

It was that kind of friendship.

CHAPTER 1

When one thinks of the Hulk, the first thing that comes to one's mind is probably *big, green angry guy who flies an Avengers Quinjet.*

Wait. That's not the first thing that comes to mind?

Well, then you must not know the Hulk.

Just a few moments ago, the Hulk had been standing on the surface of a S.H.I.E.L.D. (Strategic Homeland Intervention, Enforcement, and Logistics Division) Helicarrier—pretty much, as its name suggests, a flying aircraft carrier. The Helicarrier served as a mobile headquarters for S.H.I.E.L.D. The Hulk was on board for only a moment, just long enough to deposit Natasha Romanoff—Black Widow—on its expansive deck.

The Hulk, along with the rest of the Avengers, had been locked in a life-or-death struggle against an incredible artificial intelligence named Ultron. That the Hulk—Bruce Banner, actually—had a hand in Ultron's creation was lost neither on Banner nor his green-skinned alter ego. For unbeknownst to the rest of the Avengers, Banner and Tony Stark had been working in secret to develop a defense system that could protect Earth from almost any threat, including alien invasion. A system that, somewhat ironically, had proved in and of itself to be one of the greatest threats Earth had ever faced.

It was Tony Stark's dream, to be fair. He wanted to leave a legacy, something that would make everyone safe. The secret to this defense system—dubbed Ultron—was its artificial intelligence. The secret to *creating* this artificial intelligence had eluded both Stark and Banner. But the dream appeared to be within their grasp when Stark obtained a strange gem taken from a scepter that belonged to Loki—adopted brother to the mighty Thor. The gem made the seemingly impossible happen. Ultron came to life.

As often happens to the best-laid plans of mice and men, however, something went wrong. As Ultron sprang to sentient life, he decided that the biggest threat facing the planet was humanity itself. It took the combined might of every Avenger—the Hulk, Black Widow, Iron Man, Thor, Captain America, and Hawkeye—plus the help of two super-powered individuals, Wanda and Pietro

Maximoff, and the aid of a synthetic human known as Vision, to stop Ultron and his vast robot army.

The Hulk had channeled his anger and rage for a just cause, once again saving the people of Earth from a terrible fate. In the process, however, he—Banner—came to realize that Earth also needed to be saved…from him. Before the final battle with Ultron, the Hulk was driven into a terrible rampage by Wanda. She and her brother had briefly allied themselves with Ultron, before they understood what the artificial intelligence had planned for humanity. Wanda's powers had caused the Hulk to suffer terrible hallucinations. These hallucinations pushed the Hulk to the brink, and he was on the verge of becoming the monster that some truly believed him to be. Only Tony Stark, wearing an anti-Hulk suit made of Iron Man armor, was able to stop him.

And only Black Widow could calm down the Hulk, triggering the incredible transformation back from brute to introverted scientist.

Black Widow.

The Hulk—Banner—cared for her. For Natasha Romanoff. Perhaps too much. Certainly enough that he realized she wasn't safe around him. Not while he could turn into an out-of-control creature again. Who knows what might have happened if Stark hadn't been around to subdue the Hulk? Who might have been hurt?

It was this bleak realization that drove the Hulk to his next act. After setting Black Widow gently on the Helicarrier deck, he turned and looked one last time in his friend's eyes. A voice inside him—Banner's voice—wanted the Hulk to linger for just another moment so he could see her face a little longer.

But the Hulk knew it was time to go. He looked up into the sky as an Avengers Quinjet soared overhead.

Gamma-irradiated leg muscles tensed, then released, sending the Incredible Hulk into the air like a missile. To any human eye, it would have looked like the man-monster was flying. For all intents and purposes, he was. He had hurled himself in the direction of the Quinjet. Such was his speed that he quickly caught up with the craft. The Quinjet's rear bay was open, and the Hulk landed inside with a loud thump, causing the Quinjet to veer suddenly before recovering.

The Hulk grunted and stomped inside the Quinjet. He was unsurprised to find Ultron at the controls. The robot had transferred his artificial intelligence into another Ultron body and was using the Avengers' own transport as a means of escape.

Right after he had tried to destroy the Hulk.

Right after he had tried to destroy the Hulk's friends.

This made the Hulk angry.

"Oh, for God's sake," Ultron said, his robotic voice full of frustration, as the Hulk grabbed his metal body. With another grunt and seemingly little effort, the Hulk hurled Ultron out of the Quinjet's open bay. The robot was helpless against the Hulk's extreme power. He looked like a harmless speck of dust as he fell through empty air to his fate below. The Hulk had no idea what would happen to Ultron when he crashed back to Earth. He did know this: A fall from that height would damage Ultron's body beyond repair. He also knew that the Avengers would find what was left of him and shut him down for good.

The Hulk drew a deep breath into his mammoth lungs, held it, and exhaled. Then he heard a voice.

Her voice.

"Hey, big guy, we did it."

Black Widow. Her voice and face came in loud and clear over a Quinjet monitor. The Hulk walked slowly toward the front of the vehicle, staring at Black Widow as she spoke.

"The job is finished," she continued. Her voice cracked with emotion. "Now I need you to turn this bird around, okay?"

He could have spoken at any moment, even grunted to acknowledge that he'd heard her. Anything to let her know that he was fine, and that he would listen and come back to his team.

But that wasn't in the cards. Not today. From inside the Hulk, Banner knew he had to get away. As long as he could transform into the rampaging Hulk, no one would be safe around him—least of all, his friends.

"We can't track you in stealth mode," Black Widow said. That was true. The Quinjets were capable of traveling almost anywhere without being followed. "So help me out."

The Hulk stared at the image of Black Widow on the screen. She looked tired from the battle with Ultron. Most of all, she looked concerned for her friend. The Hulk sensed this and reached out to the screen, as if he were going to touch her hand.

"I need y—"

The Hulk gently pressed a button on the monitor, cutting off Black Widow midsentence.

Alone, the Hulk sat on the floor of the Quinjet as its engines whined, the automatic controls sending the mighty ship through Earth's upper atmosphere and into the deep unknown of space.

CHAPTER 2

One does not simply walk into the Realm of Fire.

Unless the one in question is the son of Odin. In that case, one simply *does* walk into the Realm of Fire.

Of course, there are consequences that go with so rash a decision.

"Perhaps if they called this the Realm of Eternal Summer," Thor muttered to himself, "they might have more visitors." Thor grinned. He wished someone, anyone, had been around to hear what he had said. He was sure they would have laughed. After all, Thor was quite amusing, if he did say so himself.

But there wasn't much laughter to be found here in the Realm of Fire.

Among Asgardians, it was more commonly referred to as Muspelheim, one of the Nine Realms. It was a land like nothing else. A world of eternal, ever-burning flame, where heat reigned. Water was not to be found on Muspelheim, not anywhere—in its place, bubbling pools of lava dotted the rocky landscape. The skies were rife with the stench of sulfur, and minute particles of ash constantly blew in the hot winds.

A vacation spot Muspelheim was not.

How Thor had come to be at Muspelheim was...what did Earth people like to say? It was...complicated. For the last few years, the son of Odin had been splitting his time between the realm of Asgard—his home—and Midgard. You might know it as Earth. On that world, Thor had found a sense of responsibility that had eluded him in Asgard. A responsibility to help people, those who could not otherwise help themselves. He had also found friendship and comrades in the form of the Avengers.

It would not be so bad having them for company right now, thought Thor as he plodded along the searing soil of Muspelheim. He pulled at his beard, now grown long. His garments were worn, tattered. The Thor who walked into Muspelheim was not the same polished Thor who had joined the Avengers.

The Avengers. It had been some time since Thor had fought beside his teammates. The last challenge they had faced was Ultron. The android had an agenda of extinction that he had attempted to force upon the Earth.

Alongside his teammates, Thor fought with valor befitting an Asgardian, shattering Ultron's plans once and for all.

In the middle of that epic battle, however, there had been the vision.

On the surface, the vision *seemed* to have been caused by Wanda Maximoff—she whose powers could cause a person to have incredibly realistic, disturbing hallucinations. But there was something so vivid, so real about the vision that had come to Thor—something so hellish and frightening that it disturbed him to his very core. He could not, would not believe that the vision was solely the result of another's hallucinatory powers.

In that vision, Thor glimpsed an eerie room full of Asgardians, his friend Heimdall among them. Heimdall, the so-called Watcher of Worlds, controlled the Bifrost— the bridge that allows beings to travel swiftly from Asgard to the other Realms. Thor had seen Heimdall in this vision, but Heimdall had not seen him—for the Watcher of Worlds was blind. It was clear that some awful, terrible fate had befallen the Asgardians, but what it was, Thor knew not. For as soon as the vision had come to him, it fled, banished to the shadows of his mind.

But still the vision lingered within Thor. He wondered

what it meant. It was not merely a hallucination caused by Wanda. It must have been an ill omen, a portent of something to come. A glimpse into the future of Asgard, a warning to Thor.

Perhaps that explained in part why Thor had made the possibly foolhardy decision to enter Muspelheim alone. Something about the vision had led him to this place. Something that he had seen in his mind's eye but now could not quite recall. He knew he had to be here, right now. And at least in Muspelheim he would find a welcome distraction. Something to take his mind off the vision. And what better distraction was there than walking through an inhospitable inferno filled with fire demons?

He had yet to encounter any demons, of course, but then, he had only just arrived in this fiery land. It would take the demons some time to realize that an Asgardian had dared enter Muspelheim. Thor wanted—*needed*—a battle...something that would draw his attention to the here and now, allowing him to stay in the moment. He saw not a soul as he trudged along the molten ground. Here he had gone to all the trouble to steal into the Realm of Fire, and no one had come to greet him.

"Unbelievable," Thor said out loud, and he rolled his eyes. So he did what any Asgardian who had just appeared in the flaming world of Muspelheim would do.

He introduced himself as only Thor could.

Summoning the power of the storm through Mjolnir, Thor brought down lightning from the sky to meet the scorched earth of the Realm of Fire. He did this repeatedly, causing multiple arcs of pure electricity to strafe the ground.

The sound of the thunder was deafening.

The lightning stopped. Then there was silence.

But only for a moment.

For in the distance, the savage roars of the fire demons could be heard. Closer and closer, the sound came.

Thor smiled.

CHAPTER 3

Hulk's head hurts bad," the Hulk muttered unhappily. He rubbed his skull with a thick green hand. His eyes were closed, and yet a bright light burned through his eyelids.

These were the first words the man-monster had uttered in who knew how long. Certainly, they were the first words he had spoken since before he boarded the Quinjet and tossed Ultron to the winds. Before he'd turned off his comm and cut himself off from Black Widow. From anyone on Earth who might find him. Before the Quinjet had taken the Hulk into the depths of space. Before...

The Hulk opened his eyes slowly. Harsh sunlight poured in. Quickly, he rose to his feet, still holding his head with one big hand. He took several tentative steps, pounding the ground, and immediately tripped over what looked like a giant old wheel.

For the first time, the Hulk looked at the landscape around him, and saw that he was standing in what looked like an enormous garbage dump. As far as he could see, debris from the wormholes were scattered everywhere. It fell continuously, raining trash from the universe all over the desolate ground.

Where was he? Why did his head hurt so much? Why was it so hard to think? Why did the Hulk want to think, anyway?

Wait.

The Hulk wasn't in the Quinjet? But if the Hulk wasn't in the Quinjet, what had happened? Had the vehicle crashed somehow? Had the impact knocked the Hulk unconscious?

Was he back on Earth?

The Hulk tried to remember, but that was always difficult for him. Remembering things, like thinking, was more Banner's speed. But somewhere inside the Hulk's clouded brain, there was Banner, wondering, analyzing, always the scientist.

The wormhole, Banner thought.

Banner had seen it through the Quinjet's cockpit. He'd known what it was the moment it had appeared there in space, plain as day. It was similar to a black hole, but full of color. It swirled, brilliant, beckoning. Banner knew it was a wormhole.

The Hulk? He had no idea it was called a wormhole. It was bright and colorful, and he didn't like it.

That was unfortunate, because that was exactly where the Quinjet had headed. The Quinjet had burst through the wormhole and somehow deposited the Hulk here, in this strange, unfamiliar place.

The Hulk's head still hurt, and he was tired of Banner, tired of thinking.

The green Goliath plodded along the rocky surface crowded with trash. The Hulk looked up at the sky, expecting to see the sun that had woken him up so unceremoniously. And there was a sun, to be sure. But there was also something else.

A vast array of swirling lights—like holes in the sky itself.

Wormholes, Banner thought from inside the Hulk's mind.

The Hulk grunted in assent as he watched the wormholes swirling in the sky. A steady stream of objects seemed to pour forth from them. He watched intently as all manner of debris escaped the confines of the swirling lights. Strange crafts, asteroids, satellites, and more were being perpetually ejected from the wormholes, falling down to the surface in rapid succession.

"Where Hulk?" he said, his voice bouncing off the dunes and sounding unnaturally loud, even for the Hulk.

Banner knew that he was no longer on Earth. Unlike the Hulk, he put two and two together and realized that the wormhole was a singularity. An interstellar passageway, connecting two disparate places. A "space shortcut" between worlds. The Quinjet must have passed through the wormhole and deposited him here. Wherever *here* was.

"I've got one," came a voice from beyond a piece of metal debris. It looked like a ship of some kind. It was twisted and smoking....Was it the Quinjet? The Hulk couldn't tell for certain. There were so many ships partially covered in the wasteland. It was like some kind of galactic graveyard. "I'll bring him in," said the voice.

The Hulk curled his upper lip into a savage sneer and grunted. "No one has Hulk," he scowled, and he meant it.

Then he saw her. It was a woman, her head popping over the debris, staring directly at the Hulk. She wore armor, and her arms were bare—the Hulk could see she had markings of some kind on her face. The woman started to walk forward, and as she grew closer, the Hulk could see she wore something on her hands that looked like elaborate brass knuckles.

Weapons.

Weapons meant fighting.

Fighting was something the Hulk understood.

An inhuman growl escaped the Hulk's mouth as he bounded toward the woman. Raising his right fist, the Goliath brought it down into the spot where the woman stood.

She didn't flinch as the Hulk's fist drove right into the ground in front of her. It was like she had been expecting the Hulk to do exactly that, and so stood in place. The Hulk's momentum carried him through, and he hit the ground, rolling end over end.

This made the Hulk angry.

"Fight," the Hulk snarled.

The woman started to walk forward once more, holding a fob-like device in her right hand. "Fight is exactly right," she said. "You're here to fight. The Grandmaster will make sure of that."

She advanced on the Hulk, and the man-monster balled up both fists in anger.

"Leave Hulk alone," the Hulk yelled, and he meant it.

"Oh, you'll do nicely," the woman said. "He'll pay me handsomely for what I'm going to bring him."

The Hulk was getting madder by the second, as somewhere deep inside, Banner was asking questions. Questions like *Who's the Grandmaster? Who is this woman? What is that thing in her right hand?* But the Hulk had a way of getting Banner to shut up and stop thinking and asking so many questions.

The jade giant clapped his enormous hands together and expected the woman to be blown off her feet by the resulting shock wave. But this did not happen. She hadn't moved even a millimeter. Whoever she was, she had incredible strength.

This both impressed the Hulk and made him *really* angry.

He threw another punch at the woman, but she easily ducked it. The Hulk staggered, thrown off balance. Turning around, he saw the woman waving the fob in front of his face.

Banner had realized what was going on a while ago—the woman was playing some kind of game with him. She was using the Hulk's anger against him, making him so mad that he kept slipping up. It was driving the Hulk nuts.

So when the woman waved the fob in the Hulk's face again, the Hulk was sure he had it figured out. He didn't move. He planted his heavy feet in the hot sand and did nothing as he sneered at his foe, daring her to do something.

Which she promptly did.

She activated the fob, and it fired something right at the Hulk's neck. A moment later, the Hulk's muscles tensed, his teeth began to grind uncontrollably, and the worst pain that he'd ever felt coursed through his veins like poison.

And then everything went dark.

CHAPTER 4

Y ou dare to enter Muspelheim, Asgardian?"

Thor's smile grew wider. The air around him was thick with ash as the first wave of fire demons descended, and the son of Odin couldn't have been more pleased. Thor stood his ground, legs braced, brandishing Mjolnir before him. Mjolnir, which had accompanied him into countless battles on countless worlds against countless foes.

The fire demon's voice crackled with the sound of an inferno. "None of your kind are welcome in our realm, Asgardian."

"That may be, but I was in the area and thought I might drop by for a visit," Thor said casually.

The fire demons looked at one another, not sure how to respond. Humor was not a known commodity on Muspelheim. It must have gone up in smoke, along with everything else in the Realm of Fire.

Eventually, the fire demon said, "Stay a moment longer and face death. Your own."

"Not this day," Thor shot back. He tightened his grip on Mjolnir.

And just like that, the fire demons were upon him.

A battle begins with but a single blow. In this case, it was not Thor who drew first blood, but the fire demons.

A single demon lunged for Thor, its flaming hand gripping his left arm. Thor let out a gasp of pain as the fire demon's touch seared his flesh. A sharp blow from Mjolnir dislodged the fire demon from his burning arm. Thor clasped a hand over the burn, rubbing it. He clenched his teeth. *That*, he thought, *cannot be allowed to happen again.*

Thor cast a glance at the smoldering ground, focusing on the fire demon he had just struck. When he looked up, he saw hundreds more flaming demons just waiting to attack. He gazed at the horizon, and it was fire demons as far as the eye could see.

As he had done so many times before, Thor began to hurl his hammer around his head as fast as he could. The twirling of the mallet kept the fire demons at bay, but that was not Thor's true intent. The hammer whirled faster and faster, picking up speed, until at last Thor released Mjolnir.

Like an arrow, Mjolnir flew straight and true, striking down one fire demon after another as it soared away from Thor and into the distance. The demons struck by Thor's hammer knew defeat that day. But the other demons were moronic enough to see Thor temporarily deprived of his hammer and think him easy fodder.

Fire demons could be such fools.

A moment later, Mjolnir returned to Thor's hand. Along the way, it had taken out countless more fire demons. Thor reclaimed his enchanted hammer and looked at the sea of fire before him.

Settle in, he thought. *You're going to be here awhile.*

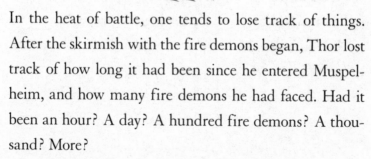

In the heat of battle, one tends to lose track of things. After the skirmish with the fire demons began, Thor lost track of how long it had been since he entered Muspelheim, and how many fire demons he had faced. Had it been an hour? A day? A hundred fire demons? A thousand? More?

Wave after wave of incendiary hordes came upon Thor as he slowly advanced along the molten surface of the Realm of Fire. Each stride brought him closer. Closer to earning the attention of the one Thor had come to see.

For he had no interest in the fire demons, other than as a diversion.

Mjolnir was in his right hand. Thor let the hammer slide loose, grabbing it by the leather thong that was attached to its grip. He held out his left hand, keeping the fire demons away from him even as they continued to advance in droves. Thor twirled the mallet once with incredible force, then released the thong. Mjolnir flew from his hand, colliding with a row of at least fifty fire demons. The hammer hit them hard, casting each aside as if they were insignificant ants.

No sooner had the hammer left his hand than it soared back, returning to its master. Thor caught Mjolnir in his right hand and surveyed his work, nodding slightly.

"I'd like to see the Hulk do better," he boasted proudly.

CHAPTER 5

The Hulk was angry, even by Hulk standards.

The thing that had hit him in the neck—whatever it was—hurt. It actually *hurt* the Hulk.

He wasn't used to things hurting, and he really wasn't used to being beaten.

So: angry.

"Hulk's whole body hurts," said the Hulk.

After the horrendous pain, the Hulk felt something else he hadn't felt before: paralyzed. He couldn't move at all. He kept telling his enormous limbs to move, to smash, but they wouldn't listen. And when the woman strapped some crazy-looking goggles over his head, the Hulk couldn't do anything to prevent it. With the goggles on, the Hulk couldn't see anything, either.

As the woman took him aboard a vehicle of some kind, he heard a voice come over the communications system. The voice called the woman Scrapper 142.

So that was who the Hulk was angry at.

Seething, the Hulk grunted as he felt the goggles being removed from his face. He could see once again. He reached a hand up to his eyes.

He could also move again.

The Hulk looked around. He was no longer standing in the wasteland with space junk all around and wormholes swirling in the sky. Scrapper 142, the angry woman who had somehow, against all odds, subdued him, was nowhere to be seen. No longer was he outside. The Hulk now stood inside what could only be described as a ring.

A fighting ring.

The Hulk rubbed his eyes, clearing them. Standing in the ring along with him were five others.

They weren't human.

Then again, was the Hulk really human? Somewhere inside him, Banner wondered.

"Welcome to Sakaar, my friend," came a voice from out of nowhere. It was loud and friendly, and the Hulk hated it. "Let's see if you'll make a worthy addition to my Contest of Champions."

The Hulk grunted. Inside, Banner had questions.

What's Sakaar? Is that the name of this place? This planet?

The five other beings in the ring were just as large and imposing as the Hulk. Some had multiple arms, some multiple legs, and they all looked ready for a fight.

"Not Hulk's friend," the green behemoth muttered.

"Oh, come now," said the disembodied voice. "I'm everyone's friend. Just ask them! Well, not everyone's. But let's not dwell on that. How about a battle? I'm willing to bet that you're quite good when it comes to fighting. You seem tailor-made for it."

So that's what's going on here, Banner thought from inside the Hulk's mind. *I'm supposed to fight with these... beings. It's a game of some kind.*

The Hulk sneered again, his lip curling in what appeared to be a smile. A fighting game was one he knew how to win.

"What manner of creature is this?!" screamed a four-armed alien as it landed face-first on the ground. A second later, a heavy, wide green foot stepped on its back, causing the four-armed alien to yelp in pain. "Where did you find this thing?!"

From the moment the six-way battle had begun, the Hulk was squarely in his element. To say that he was evenly matched or that this competition was remotely close would have been one big gamma-irradiated lie. The Hulk was absolutely mopping the floor with his competitors. Though each one was roughly his size (or larger), and each one possessed incredible strength, the Hulk was better. He was stronger.

Strongest one there is, thought the Hulk.

The Hulk was like a kid in a candy store—he hardly knew which opponent to fight next. They all looked so easy to defeat! An eight-foot-tall beast of an alien snarled at the Hulk, thick drool dripping from its fangs. That was all the invitation the Hulk needed.

The green-skinned Goliath rammed a clenched fist into the beast's belly, knocking it flat on its behind. The beast yowled in pain and spat out words in a language the Hulk had never heard before. It sounded like cursing to the Hulk. He didn't like it. So he lifted the beast over his head and threw it right into one of his other opponents.

The beast collided with a six-legged insect-like creature, and both went down for the count.

"Fight," commanded the Hulk as he stared at his

remaining opponents. In the heat of battle, a thought occurred to Banner: *The Hulk is enjoying this. He's actually enjoying this.*

"Fight!" snarled the Hulk once more. As if in answer, an amorphous orange blob oozed from behind the Hulk, covering him in an instant. For a moment, the Hulk was surprised—he found himself enveloped in a viscous goo, unable to breathe. He tried to punch his way out. But the orange blob stretched with the Hulk's fist as he punched, and snapped back. It clung tightly to the Hulk and wouldn't let go.

This *really* made the Hulk angry.

And so he pounded the floor with both fists. The resulting shock wave caused the ring to shake. Still, the orange blob held fast. So the Hulk hit the floor again. And again. And again. The whole room was shaking, and slowly, too, was the orange blob. The vibrations from the Hulk's thunderous blows started to cause breaks in the goo. The Hulk was now able to breathe. He thrust both arms back as fast as he could and threw the orange blob off his body. The creature landed with a loud *THWUCK*.

The Hulk punched it, and the blob splattered into a hundred smaller, inert blobs.

The scaly-skinned creature was the only one left. For its part, the creature seemed almost reluctant to fight—it had seen what it was up against, and maybe decided getting smashed wasn't exactly worth the effort. But there was nothing the creature could do as the Hulk ran directly toward it, his fists knocking the lizard-like being off its feet. Scales sprayed into the air as the Hulk knocked the creature back. The alien collapsed, landing in a heap on the floor.

Elapsed time from the start of the Hulk's battle to his victory over five alien competitors: two minutes, ten seconds.

The Hulk turned his head from left to right, looking at his fallen competitors. They were all still alive, and all shaking their heads, wondering what—or more precisely, who—had happened to them.

The Hulk found himself wishing he had someone else to punch.

Then came a sound. Something unexpected that got the Hulk's attention.

It was…applause. Applause could be heard inside the ring. The Hulk jerked his head up, looking around. From out of the darkness, a tall being wearing garish robes stepped forward. He smiled at the Hulk as he continued to clap his elegant, slim hands.

"That was masterful, absolutely masterful," he burbled enthusiastically. "Really. You are going to make quite the addition to my Contest of Champions. In fact, I think you might even be *the* Champion one of these days. Perhaps my most precious Champion."

The Hulk snorted. "Who?" the Hulk said curtly. Did the question come from him or Banner? He didn't know.

"Ah, yes, where are my manners?" the being said, as if in response. He had a blue streak that ran over his bottom lip down his chin. Placing his left hand on his chest, he said, "I'm the Grandmaster. And you are…"

"Leaving," said the Hulk, and he started to walk away from the Grandmaster. He didn't see a door right away, but there had to be one around somewhere.

"I wouldn't do that if I were you," the Grandmaster said. His tone wasn't at all threatening. In fact, it sounded full of concern.

The Hulk took one more step before his world filled with a white-hot pain he had felt once before, in the wasteland. It was as if the pain of every single transformation he had experienced, every time he'd gone from

Banner to the Hulk and back, had been compacted and distilled into this one moment. The Hulk crumpled to the ground, writhing.

"See, I told you not to do that, and then *that* happened," the Grandmaster said. "You're wearing an Obedience Disk now, my friend. I wish it wasn't necessary, but, well, you can see how it is."

As the pain began to subside, the Hulk put one big green hand on the side of his neck. That must be what Scrapper 142 had used to subdue the Hulk in the first place. In all the chaos that ensued after, he hadn't noticed anything attached to his body. Well, he certainly noticed the small, circular mechanical device attached to his neck now. *This is how they'll control us*, Banner thought from within. The Hulk didn't want to think.

The Hulk wanted to smash.

He grabbed the Obedience Disk, and received another terrible jolt of pain for his trouble.

"Oh, now, now, don't grab it," said the Grandmaster. "Don't ever grab it. That's going to be quite painful as well." He wasn't gloating at all. Rather, he actually seemed concerned for the Hulk's welfare. "Best to leave it alone and listen. I think we have a great deal to offer you, and you certainly have a great deal to offer us. Me, I mean. You seem to like smashing things, yes?"

That got the Hulk's attention. He looked up at the Grandmaster and cocked his head slightly.

"Ah, yes, I assumed so. Then you'll definitely like it here. I can offer you almost unlimited opportunity to smash. In return, you fight before adoring crowds. I mean, they'll love you. What's not to love about you? You're big, you're green, you smash things. What do you say? Stay here and fight for me on the planet Sakaar, and be hailed as a true Champion."

Wait. What? What is going on here? Banner thought.

But the Hulk didn't want to think. He liked what he heard.

"Hulk stay ... for now."

CHAPTER 6

The fight continued for hours. Thor, encountering what had to be armies upon armies of fire demons, made his way across a scorched, perpetual battlefield. The clashes were serving their purpose, for Thor was certainly distracted from his disturbing visions.

The visions. Something he had glimpsed in those unsettling visions had brought Thor to this infernal place.

"Have at thee!" Thor shouted, his lungs burning as he drew in the scalding air of Muspelheim. Another wave of fire demons threw themselves upon the son of Odin. It seemed like he could keep at this all day, a thought that reminded Thor of his fellow Avenger, Captain America. That was something the Super-Soldier liked to say when things were at their bleakest and it seemed like he might lose the fight—*I could do this all day*. Thor smiled as he continued to hurl fire demons away from him.

"Are you mad, Asgardian?" a fire demon screeched at Thor. "Even if you defeat us all, you have earned the wrath eternal of Surtur! He will pull the flesh from your bones while you writhe in agony!"

It hit Thor like a bolt of lightning from mighty Mjolnir itself.

Not the fire demon's threat. That did not concern the son of Odin. No, it was the name that the fire demon had mentioned that had awoken the memory within Thor.

Surtur.

The absolute ruler of Muspelheim.

In the midst of battle, Thor now remembered why he had come to Muspelheim. He remembered a figure he had glimpsed in his visions, someone...some*thing* that sat at the center of them.

Surtur.

Thor smiled once more, standing up straight, like a king.

"I would have a word with your master!" Thor called. "Tell Surtur I have come for him! Will he not face me? Or is your lord and master afraid of one Asgardian?" He wasn't sure if his boastful taunt could be heard above the din of fire demons and roaring flames of Muspelheim.

So he decided to get Surtur's attention.

Raising Mjolnir toward the heavens, Thor once more channeled the power of the storm itself and called for nature to do his bidding. The sky rumbled with thunder, and lightning cascaded from the roiling clouds above. It struck the ground everywhere, or so it seemed. Fire demons far and wide were racked with electricity. They flailed, unable to stop it, unable to do anything but succumb to the Asgardian's relentless assault.

Then the impossible happened. Something that had never before occurred in Muspelheim. Something Surtur himself could never have predicted.

It began to rain.

In the Realm of Fire.

A torrential downpour, summoned by Thor.

The driving rain hit the ground so hard that it stung even Thor's body. It pummeled the harsh terrain of Muspelheim unforgivingly. Great clouds of steam formed, making it almost impossible for Thor to see his foes, or anything else, for that matter.

And then—the screams.

The screams of the fire demons, experiencing an agony they had never felt before. The agony of endless rain eating away at their fiery bodies.

Once more, Thor cried out, "Tell Surtur I have come for him!"

CHAPTER 7

Yo're next for processing. Follow me."

The Hulk heard the voice and walked through the dimly lit hallway into a large room. On every wall, as far as he could see, were weapons. Armor. All kinds, all shapes, all sizes. There were axes and spears and hammers and scythes and bludgeons and truncheons and helmets and shields and on and on. Some looked familiar to the Hulk, very much like Earth armaments. Others were completely alien to him—in fact, they probably were alien. He thought he recognized some weapons that the Chitauri had used in their attempted invasion of New York.

What was this place?

As if in answer, a hefty alien wearing a leather apron greeted the jade giant. He looked up at the Hulk. He looked down at the Hulk. He did it again.

Wash, rinse, repeat.

"I am here to arm you for your upcoming match," said the alien in the leather apron.

The Hulk grunted.

"Something tells me that you don't need a weapon."

The Hulk shook his head in agreement. "Hulk is weapon."

"I'm sure. Still, take this," the alien in the leather apron said, holding out a huge battle-axe. The axe had two blades: On one side, a small one ended in a sharp point; on the other was a much larger blade with jagged teeth. The alien tried to shove it into the Hulk's hands.

The green Goliath made no effort to raise his hands and take the axe.

"Hulk *is* weapon," he repeated.

The alien all but rolled his eyes and pressed a button on the device he was carrying.

For the third time that day, the Hulk learned what it meant to wear an Obedience Disk. If he was the strongest one there was, then this was the worst pain there was.

The Obedience Disk crackled as the Hulk roared in agony. As soon as it started, it stopped.

"Take this," the alien said, motioning to the battle-axe in his hands.

The Hulk drew in a deep breath and picked up the axe. He sneered at the alien, grunting.

Stay calm, Banner thought from inside the Hulk.

Don't want to stay calm, the Hulk thought. *Want to smash*.

"I've seen that look before a hundred times," said a voice as the Hulk heard someone enter the room. "A thousand times. Probably more than that. You want to hit him. Save it. Use it in the battle to come."

The Hulk grunted as he saw a woman walking toward him. A woman with a marked face, wearing armor.

The angry woman. The one they called Scrapper 142.

"The Grandmaster has a lot of faith in you," she said. "He's betting that you might become the new Champion."

The Hulk stared at Scrapper 142. "Why Angry Girl here?" he said, turning his attention back to the battle-axe he didn't want but was being forced to take.

Scrapper 142 smiled at the moniker. "I also think you have the makings of a Champion," she said. "I thought you should know that before you entered the arena."

With that, the woman turned around and left.

CHAPTER 8

As swiftly as Thor had brought the driving, punishing rains to Muspelheim, he banished them. By his command, and through Mjolnir's will, the rains ceased. The screams of the fire demons subsided.

For a brief moment, no fire demon dared attack the son of Odin. Not when they realized what power he wielded, and could wield again, if he so chose.

So he said, for the last time, quite calmly, "Surtur. Take me to him."

The fire demons grew silent, wary of the Asgardian, and stared at him suspiciously. They must have realized that the game they were playing with Thor was a zero-sum one.

And now they must be communicating with their master, he thought, satisfied.

Suddenly, Thor was struck with yet another terrible vision. He closed his eyes against the intruding images, not wanting to show weakness in front of the fire demons. Thor knew in the core of his being that the visions were an omen, a herald of things to come. He would know more of this vision. And Surtur's role in it.

But why? What was the lord of this fiery realm doing in these awful visions that plagued him so?

Thor breathed out in relief as, slowly, the vision subsided, leaving him shaken but upright. He didn't know what these visions meant. But he would have answers. And only Surtur could provide them.

What happened next was completely predictable and yet wholly unexpected.

The predictable: The fire demons had, in fact, communed with Surtur—or rather, Surtur had communed with the fire demons—and Surtur had demanded that the son of Odin be brought before his presence.

Of course, Thor knew that he would not be received as a "special envoy" from Asgard, afforded all the comforts of a diplomat. Not after the way he had entered Muspelheim. Not after the battles and vanquished fire demons. Not after the driving rain. No, the only way he would see Surtur would be as a prisoner.

The wholly unexpected: This was exactly what Thor wished.

"You belong to Surtur now," crackled a fire demon, who beckoned Thor forward. "He will grant you audience. In turn, you shall be his prisoner until you die."

Thor nodded. "I shall come along quietly, then. Do you have handcuffs or…?" He extended both arms, offering up his wrists to the fire demons as if the demons were the police and he a common thief. They looked at Thor, then at one another, not understanding. Handcuffs were likely not exactly standard issue in Muspelheim, Thor thought, enjoying his joke.

"The hammer," said a fire demon, gesturing at Mjolnir. "Surrender the hammer."

"Yes, can't have an armed man going to see Surtur." Thor knelt down and placed Mjolnir on the ground. "I'll see you soon," he said to the enchanted mallet, giving it a tender pat as one would a treasured pet.

As Thor began to trail after the fire demons toward Surtur—and his fate—he heard a commotion behind him that caused him to look over his shoulder. A number of fire demons had raced over to Mjolnir and were each trying in turn to lift the mallet. They struggled and pulled and tugged and failed in their efforts.

For only one who was truly worthy could lift Mjolnir.

It was just as Thor wanted.

As he traversed the searing soil, surrounded by silent, sparking fire demons on all sides, Thor had a good deal of time to think. When he wasn't dwelling on Surtur and the vision, he thought about his life, what he had been doing with it. Ever since he had arrived on Midgard and made friends on that world, he had been both an Avenger and heir to the Asgardian throne and protector of the Nine Realms. Sometimes he was the dutiful son of Odin, helping his fellow Asgardians through their trials and tribulations. His adopted brother, Loki, saw to it that there were troubles aplenty. Loki, the Trickster. Master of lies and deceit. How many problems had he caused for Thor, his family, and his friends?

Loki had been the catalyst that brought the Avengers together in the first place, Thor remembered.

The Avengers. More and more, Thor had been spending his time on Earth with the Avengers. Their problems became his problems. Their battles, his battles. Their victories, his victories.

The team…their friendship…meant more to him than they could possibly know.

Still…

Thor felt something else. It wasn't a feeling he was used to, and it wasn't one he necessarily liked. The pangs of guilt. He felt guilty. Guilty for the time he'd spent away from Asgard and his brethren. As the rightful heir to the Asgardian throne, should he not have been by his father's side, instead of fighting beside the people of Midgard? What would Odin think? Were Thor's increasingly frequent absences the cause of the terrible visions?

He wiped the sweat from his brow and continued the long march to see Surtur. Thor swore he would have his answers yet.

CHAPTER 9

The Hulk could hardly believe what he saw.

There he was, stranded on an alien world—Sakaar—standing in the middle of an enormous arena. Bigger than any stadium he had ever seen on Earth. As he turned his head and looked around, he saw an endless sea of beings sitting in rows upon rows of seats. There were some humans scattered among the crowd (at least, beings who appeared to be human), but mostly he saw faces that clearly belonged to beings from the farthest reaches of space. And all these beings were cheering. They were hungry. Hungry for entertainment.

And in the middle of it all stood the Incredible Hulk.

Raising his head skyward, the Hulk saw great starships that appeared to hover directly above the arena. Above that, of course, were the ubiquitous wormholes, brilliant, swirling, ejecting junk on the distant horizon.

And then there was the sixty-foot-tall alien clad in elegant robes, standing in front of him. This confused the Hulk. How had the Grandmaster become so huge? From inside, Banner realized this must be a projection of some kind—a way for the Grandmaster to communicate to the huge crowd and enforce his will.

The Hulk just wondered why he was so big.

"Friends!" called the Grandmaster, and the crowds cheered even louder. Their voices were as one, roaring in the Hulk's ears.

"We have a new arrival to our Contest of Champions! The Hulk...of Earth!"

Again, the crowds roared.

What is this? Banner thought from inside the Hulk.

"Will he be able to defeat"—the Grandmaster paused for dramatic effect—"our Champion from Chitauri Prime?"

That was when the Hulk saw it. A burly, ripped, cyborg-like creature holding two long staves. He was easily the same size as the Hulk. Striding into the arena, the creature manipulated the staves in wide circles. He was putting on a show for the crowd, and they loved it. The cheers grew louder.

The Hulk wasn't distracted by the cheers. He stared at his opponent.

Now the Hulk *really* wanted to smash.

An encouraging roar rose up from the crowd as the Chitauri landed yet another blow against the Hulk.

The Hulk gritted his teeth and popped up again from the ground where he'd fallen. The noise that came from the crowd would have deafened an ordinary human. But the Hulk was not an ordinary human. His gamma-irradiated body was testament to that. The green Goliath could tell who the people were cheering for, and it wasn't him. The Chitauri alien that he now faced must have been a favorite, for the crowds went wild every time he struck the Hulk with one of his staves.

Which was happening more often than the Hulk would have liked, surprisingly.

Whenever the Chitauri landed even a glancing blow, the staves sparked and sent jolts of pure agony through the Hulk's nervous system. It felt like the Obedience Disk, only slightly less painful.

The Hulk hated the staves.

He hated the Chitauri even more.

If he could just get the staves away from the Chitauri,

then the Hulk would smash and that would be the end of that.

WHAM! The Chitauri hit the Hulk right in his solar plexus, knocking the jade giant onto his knees yet again. The crowd went wild.

The Hulk struggled to his feet and faced his foe once more.

Gotta be smart about this, thought Banner.

Gotta smash, thought the Hulk.

The Hulk roared, a sound that, for a split second, rose above the din of the crowd and shocked the raucous audience into momentary silence. Then he brandished his battle-axe in both hands. What he did next was unexpected. He snapped the axe in two and flung the pieces away. The axe was getting him nowhere. He didn't like using it when he could use his fists instead.

The Chitauri warrior saw this as an opening. He raced toward the Hulk, twirling a stave in each hand. As he advanced, the Hulk clapped his massive hands together. The resulting force caught the unsuspecting Chitauri warrior off guard and threw him backward. Before he knew what was happening, the Chitauri was flat on his back in the arena, with the Hulk towering over him. The

Hulk was on him. He grabbed the two staves and threw them into the air.

They didn't come down.

At least, not anywhere near the arena.

Then the Hulk picked up the Chitauri warrior and threw *him* into the air.

He didn't come down, either.

The Hulk whirled around, looking at the crowd, grunting. The masses remained silent.

"Fantastic," came a booming voice that filled the arena. "Fantastic! The victor is...the Hulk of Earth!"

Then the cheering started once more. Slowly at first. Then the sound grew and grew as people from all over the stadium rose to their feet, applauding their new fighting hero.

The Hulk realized that the crowds were cheering for him.

Not for Banner.

For the Hulk.

The man-monster felt something inside, something he had never felt before. He felt, at last, like he belonged.

The Hulk smiled.

He was finally home.

EPILOGUE

BEFORE

BEFORE ULTRON

BEFORE SAKAAR, BEFORE MUSPELHEIM

BEFORE THE HULK'S SELF-IMPOSED EXILE

It was night, and the Avengers had gathered at Stark Tower. There was no official business this evening, no world that needed saving. It was just a chance to share a meal and each other's company. As the others gathered around, Thor found himself looking out a window that loomed large over the city of New York.

"It's not Asgard, but it's still impressive, right?"

Thor turned his head to see Bruce Banner standing next to him. The scientist smiled warmly, and Thor returned it.

"Very much so. It's just as beautiful, in its own way," Thor replied. He turned back to the window and then looked at Banner once more. "You know, Banner, there is something I've been wanting to ask you since the Battle of New York."

Banner took a long pull from the bottle of water he had in his hand. "What's on your mind?"

"I'm not sure what you recall from your time as the Hulk. We were fighting the Chitauri, you and I. Riding atop the back of a great flying beast."

Banner looked upward, as if searching his memory. "Vaguely…"

"Do you recall us smashing through the wall of Grand Central Terminal?" Thor asked.

Banner continued to look upward. "Vaguely…"

"And do you remember our victory over the creature?"

Banner shook his head. "To be honest, my memory gets a little fuzzy where the Hulk's concerned."

Thor sighed. "Well, then. There's no point in asking my next question."

Banner gave Thor a sincere look. "No, ask. Come on, before everyone gets here and this party goes full-on Stark."

"Very well. It's just I assume, based on your vague recollections, that you have no memory of punching me clear across the station."

Banner shook his head again. "No," he said. "No, I remember that like it just happened. *Wham!* You went flying." The scientist laughed a little to himself.

Thor was incredulous. "How is it that you can remember that, but you have only the vaguest recall of everything else?"

The scientist shrugged. "Maybe I only remember the good times."

Banner smiled at Thor, and the two men laughed and clinked their glasses.

THOR

SKURGE

LOKI

VALKYRIE

HELA

HEIMDALL

THE GRANDMASTER

THE HULK